ChangelingPress.com

DungeonCrawl

Mychael Black

DungeonCrawl

Mychael Black

ISBN: 978-1-60521-830-4

Publisher:
Changeling Press LLC
315 N. Centre St.
Martinsburg, WV 25404
ChangelingPress.com

Printed in the U.S.A.

Editor: Crystal Esau
Cover Artist: Angela Knight

The individual stories in this anthology have been previously released in E-Book format.

Table of Contents

Loading, Please Wait (DungeonCrawl 1)

Mychael Black

Gamer Elijah Burrows is a self-professed loner. Disowned by his parents for being gay, he takes solace in his video games. Out of all his favorites, his newest one -- DungeonCrawl -- is swiftly rising to take the number one spot for him.

When a lightning strike hits his house, knocking out the power, Elijah is anything but happy. Lack of electricity is the last thing he's worried about the second he steps foot out his front door.

What happens when a gamer finds himself stuck in the world of his fantasies? And how the hell does he survive without the aid of a mouse and keyboard?

Prologue

Elian Surgis crouched behind a boulder, shielded by a decaying tree trunk on one side and a copse of thorny bushes on the other. Bow drawn tight, he watched the guard pace back and forth. The timing had to be perfect.

If Elian missed the shot, guards would pour out of the woodwork. He'd come this far without being seen. Times like this, he wished he'd learned magic. At least then he could turn himself invisible, sneak in and steal the damn jewel without anyone knowing he'd ever been there.

Well, wishing wouldn't do him any good now. He was here and he had a job to do. Hell, he loved his work, but he was sorely tempted to put an arrow through the forehead of the next merchant or noble who asked him to retrieve some lost item in a place infested with enemies. Why couldn't they ever ask him to do something simple, like… wash their dog?

A second guard wandered out onto the narrow walkway, stopped, then turned and headed back into the tower. It was now or never. Elian loosed the arrow. The first guard jerked against the tree he'd been standing in front of, the arrow protruding from his head. No one had seen a thing.

Elian readied his next arrow. The patrolling guard came out again. Elian released his second shot. The arrow slammed into the guard's neck and sent him tumbling over the edge. A third guard ran out, sword drawn, and scanned the surroundings.

"Who's there?" he shouted.

Elian snorted to himself. Right. Like he'd stand up and announce his presence. He nocked another arrow and shot the third guard. The man dropped to the ground in front of the first one. Three down, probably two or three more to go.

Elian waited a moment to be sure no one else would emerge from the tower. He ignored the dead guards, reached the doorway, and flattened himself against the stone wall. When he peered around, he didn't see anyone. Most towers had at least five guards, which meant the others were upstairs.

Convinced it was safe, he left his hiding place and snuck around bushes, trees and rocks, edging toward the structure. The jewel he needed was in a locked box somewhere inside.

He slipped into the ground floor room. Barrels and sacks of what he assumed were drink and food sat along the walls. A part of him wanted to check them to see if they held anything remotely of value, but that would have to wait.

He started up the wooden stairs, arrow at the ready. Thank the gods he'd been working on his sneaking abilities. As he neared the top, he spotted metal boots. He lifted his bow and aimed for the guard's neck -- the only vital place not covered by metal.

Footsteps sounded. Elian shot fast. The guard landed on the floor, and Elian barely had another arrow notched before a second guard rounded the corner.

"Hey!"

Elian fired, but the guard knocked the arrow away with his sword. Elian tossed his bow down and drew both daggers off his hips. The guard slammed into him, and they tumbled down the few steps to the ground floor. Elian kneed the guard, whose sword came dangerously close to Elian's head for comfort.

The guard howled in pain, rolling away. Elian leapt up and threw one dagger. It lodged in the guard's throat. The man's eyes widened, and he made a grotesque gurgling sound. Elian grabbed the guard's discarded sword and drove it through the man's chest. Never let it be said he made a guy suffer, even if said guy had tried to behead him.

Elian retrieved his dagger and wiped the blood off on a burlap bag. He sheathed both daggers, picked up his bow and headed up the steps slowly. He peered around the corner at the top and breathed in relief. No more guards. The chest he needed sat against a far wall. Elian pulled a lock-pick from the pouch hanging from his belt and knelt down in front of the chest.

The lock refused to cooperate, of course. The pick broke. Elian grumbled and tossed it aside before pulling out another one. Thank the gods he had an abundance of them. This time the lock clicked and fell open. Elian stuck the pick back into his bag and lifted the box lid.

A bundle of cloth lay inside, tied with twine. Elian undid the knot and spread out the cloth. A red, oval-cut jewel shimmered, reflecting his young face back at him.

He re-tied the twine and stuffed the wrapped jewel into his bag. Then he began rifling through the dead guards' belongings for anything of use. He found several lock-picks, a small sack of gold coins and bits of clothing. He left the clothes but took everything else of value that wasn't nailed down.

Getting back to town wouldn't be easy. Darkness had already set in, which meant the roads would be littered with bandits. Of course, technically he was one as well, but he managed -- so far, anyway -- to keep his rather clandestine activities a secret from the city guards. He left the tower, bow once more at the ready.

Time to get the jewel to its rightful owner. There was a tavern bed with his name on it.

Chapter One

Thunder shook the windows and startled the ever-loving hell out of Elijah Burrows. He paused the game and went to look outside. The rain hadn't even started and lightning already flashed nearby, lighting up the night sky. He sighed. He loved storms, but this area was notorious for power grid issues during heavy lightning.

He wandered back over to his desk, saved his game and exited the program. At least he wouldn't lose his progress. The quest he'd been on was annoying, to say the least, but it was a necessary step along the main story line.

DungeonCrawl had only been out for a week, and Elijah couldn't tear himself away from it. The dynamic world reminded him of games like Skyrim and several massive multiplayer games he'd played over the years. He'd often wondered what life would be like in one of those games. It had to be better than his life right now, in this world.

He opened up a browser and checked his email. Most of it was junk, with the occasional digest from one gaming group or another mixed in. He scanned the messages, clicking the checkbox to delete each one as he went. He stopped and stared at one message from an address he never expected to see again. Almost dreading to read it, he opened it up anyway.

Elijah,
I received word that you were spotted in one of… those places. As per our arrangement, you were to never show your face in such a way. It reflects poorly on me and Delilah. If you expect

to continue receiving financial assistance, then you will refrain from drawing attention to yourself. My reputation is of paramount importance, and Delilah will be ostracized from her social circle should anyone discover our connection to you. Cease and desist immediately.

-- Edmond Burrows, Esq.

Elijah couldn't hit delete fast enough.

He'd been so careful to avoid cameras and anyone who he thought might know the Burrows. He'd stopped calling them his parents two years ago when they'd announced his lifestyle did not suit theirs or their expectations. The pain of them paying him to become a recluse had worn off, but no amount of money helped the loneliness.

Being the only child of the city's most prominent politician had once held perks beyond imagining. Now Elijah wished he'd been adopted. How the fuck could he be related to such cretins?

He closed the browser and sighed. No point in thinking about it now. The "financial assistance" paid for everything -- food, clothing, bills. He was still surprised they'd put him in a house they owned. What would the neighbors say if they knew he was a dirty, disgusting, sinning homosexual?

Oh, and celibate. Hell, at this rate, Elijah figured he'd reverted to being a virgin all over again.

Another boom of thunder shook the house, and lightning struck swiftly after. Elijah started shutting down the computer. The last thing he needed was to fry the damn thing. It was his only solace.

Just as soon as the screen went black, the rest of the house did, too.

"Damn it!"

Elijah grabbed his cell phone and turned on the flashlight app. He made his way carefully through the pitch black living room, praying the light from his phone found the furniture before his bare feet did.

When he reached the kitchen, he rummaged for matches and a candle in one of the junk drawers. He'd been raised to always be prepared -- probably the only good thing to come out of his childhood. He found a candle and nestled the short taper in one of the empty silver candlesticks on the dining room table. After lighting it, he turned off the phone app.

Rain pounded the windows. It looked like the Biblical Flood outside as water turned the normally pristine yard into a swamp. More thunder rumbled and lightning lit up the sky. Elijah went to the front door and opened it.

He nearly dropped the candle. "What... the... fuck?"

Elijah stared at the world beyond his front door. Last he checked, he lived in a cul-de-sac in a glitzy neighborhood.

This was not a neighborhood.

Trees surrounded the house and moonlight shone through the canopy, casting pockets of silvery light on the forest floor. Nocturnal animals moved around, unseen but heard, going about their usual night routines. Elijah wandered a few feet from the house, onto a well-worn footpath wet from rain. The trail led deeper into the woods. When he turned, the candle hit the ground, snuffed out by damp leaves.

The house he'd lived in for two years was gone. In its place stood a log cabin, small and looking quite rough. Elijah risked a glance down and exhaled in relief. His clothes, at least, remained the same.

None of this made sense. Not one bit. Maybe he was dreaming. Maybe the lightning hit the house and fried his brain. That had to be it.

There was no other explanation for why he now stood in a rundown log cabin, in the middle of the woods. No electricity, no plumbing, and...

A sinking feeling settled in his stomach.

... no computer.

"Okay, okay," Elijah muttered. He grabbed the candle and candlestick off the ground. "Get yourself together, man. There's a perfectly logical explanation. Lucid dreaming. Yeah."

He approached the cabin and peered inside. Nothing and no one. At least he had that much going for him. He stepped in and shut the wooden door. A single latch on the wall seemed to be the only thing resembling a lock so he flipped it, hooking it over a metal pin on the door itself. Then he turned to face the empty room.

Well, not quite empty. Wooden furniture sat around the relatively cozy space: a bed with fur blankets, a single dresser, a small table beside the bed, a round dining table with two stocky chairs, and various crates and barrels. A fire blazed in the fireplace, and an iron pot hung by a thick metal rod, suspended over the flames.

Elijah set the candlestick on the dining table and knelt down in front of one of the crates. The box was filled with dishes: wooden plates, dented metal cups, metal utensils. He rummaged through the contents and found several books buried beneath the mundane items. He picked up the books and sat cross-legged in front of the fire, his back to it.

He had no idea who owned the books -- or the whole cabin, for that matter. With the warmth of the fire chasing away the chill of the rain, he studied the covers of the books. Maybe one of them would tell him where he was. Most of them had symbols but no text on the outside. When he opened one that had no symbols at all, his heart nearly stopped.

An image of an eye in the center of a labyrinth stared up at him. Elijah swallowed. He knew that symbol. Hand shaking, he turned the first page and read the words a part of him had dreaded to see: *Treatise on the Labyrinthine Cult.*

He knew this book.

He'd stolen it… as Elian Surgis. He'd swiped the damn thing from a lord's library, in Calen's Rock Hold. Elijah snapped the book shut. He had to be dreaming. There was no other explanation for why he held a book he'd pilfered in a video game.

Chapter Two

Cold woke Elijah and he blinked the last edges of sleep from his eyes. God, what a fucked up dream. He'd been in a cabin tucked into the woods of...

He stared up at rough timbers. His house had spackle on the ceiling. Not bare, aged wood.

Oh, God. It was real.

He rolled his head and glanced at the room, belatedly realizing he was on the floor. He didn't remember falling asleep. The fire had died out overnight, which explained the chill.

Elijah sat up and shivered. A T-shirt, jeans and bare feet wouldn't cut it. The land of Timiria -- the world of the game DungeonCrawl -- was half-frozen. He got up and went to the single dresser near the bed. If he was going to explore and try to figure out what happened, then he couldn't walk around wearing what he currently had on.

The dresser contained several pieces of clothing, and Elijah held up a pair of black linen pants. They looked a bit big, but they'd have to do. He searched another drawer and found a pale brown shirt with laces on the front. In the last drawer, he discovered a pair of battered black leather boots. No underwear and no socks. Then again, in all the games he'd ever played, he couldn't recall ever seeing socks.

He stripped and dressed as quickly as possible in the frigid air of the cabin. Then he sat on the bed -- momentarily surprised by its actual softness -- and shoved his feet into the boots. It felt bizarre wearing them without socks, but he had the feeling it would soon be the least of his worries.

Next on the to-do list: money. And, most likely, a

weapon. From his time spent playing the game, he knew Timiria to be rather inhospitable outside of the major cities. Hell, even some of the cities weren't particularly welcoming. He wondered how many of the characters he'd met in the game actually existed in this version of Timiria. He hadn't played long enough to make a lot of friends with the game characters, and he had no idea if anyone would think him to be Elian Surgis. Did Elian even exist in this world?

Considering Elian was technically a criminal, Elijah decided against using the name, just in case. He figured his own name of Elijah would work as well as any other. If anything, no one had a clue who Elijah Burrows was, so he wasn't likely to find his name plastered on wanted posters.

He checked one of the other crates and found a small pouch tucked under several threadbare blankets and more books. When he opened the bag, he grinned. He dumped the gold coins onto the floor and counted them. Fifty. He had no idea how far that much would go, but it was better than nothing. He put them back in the pouch and set it aside. He removed the blankets and books from the crate and spotted a thin rope attached to the bottom. Curious, he tugged it. The false bottom of the crate lifted, revealing four daggers, a short bow, and two quivers of arrows.

He couldn't remember putting them down there in the game. Then again, he didn't remember this cabin either. But other things he did recognize -- namely the books -- littered the place. When he played DungeonCrawl, stealing books had turned into an obsession. Books and jewels, at any rate. Though he hadn't found any jewels yet tucked away in any of the crates.

Elijah took out the weapons and dug through the

dresser beside him again for a belt. He found one in the back of the bottom drawer, slipped the loops of the dagger sheathes over the belt, and secured the belt around his waist. He got the quiver situated with the strap diagonally across his chest, and picked up the bow. He hadn't shot one since his early teens. He turned until he faced a wide spot of bare wall. If he was going to step foot outside, he needed to remember how to do this. He drew an arrow, nocked it and aimed at a knot in the wood.

The arrow hit the wall several inches from its intended target. Elijah grumbled and took another shot. This time, the damn thing bounced off the wall and hit the floor. The third arrow, at least, missed its mark by only an inch. Christ, he couldn't remember archery being this damn hard. He fired another arrow and grinned when the tip embedded in almost dead-center of the knot. It was a start.

Several minutes and countless shots later, Elijah figured he had at least a passing chance of not dying once he went outside. He retrieved the arrows and stuck them all into the quiver. He grabbed the second quiver from the crate and then replaced the books and blankets. Time to see what lay beyond the door.

Elijah stood in the doorway and gazed out at the woods beyond the cabin. The air smelled crisp and clean, not like a modern city and its pollution. Instead of cars and radios and people, Elijah reveled in the sounds of animals and the wind blowing through the trees overhead.

He pulled the door closed and started down the trail he'd spotted last night. He had no idea where it would lead him, but he had gold and weapons and what he figured was a rudimentary knowledge of the world of Timiria already. He just needed a map. Once he had one, he could sort out where to go first.

Half an hour of walking later, Elijah stopped when the path ended at a wider road. Ruts ran along the dirt from what he assumed to be wagons. Horse hoof prints kept in line with the ruts. He bent and studied the hoof prints. It took a moment, but he finally figured out which way they went. Mud had obscured them, for the most part. He headed down the road in the direction the tracks led. Most wagons, from his game experience, served as either transportation or were used by merchants.

Elijah followed the ruts and hoof prints for what felt like several miles before he spied a wall in the distance. As he neared it, he realized it was twice as tall as himself and made of thick timbers. Towers stood at intervals along the length, and Elijah thought he saw guards in each of them. There was no gatehouse, but two guards stood at either side of the gate itself. When Elijah approached it, cautious, the guards merely watched him.

The gate opened, and Elijah walked through it. The town bustled with people and animals. Shopkeepers swept their doorsteps and announced their wares to passers-by. Kids ran after dogs, while the dogs chased after chickens. Every once in a while, a shopkeeper shouted at the whole gaggle before returning to work. No one batted an eye as Elijah made his way through the throng of market-goers. Men and women, dressed much like himself, milled about, paying him no attention whatsoever. While most of them wore only the occasional small knife on a belt, Elijah noticed a few who wore swords at their hips or bows over one shoulder. He didn't feel so out of place.

"Excuse me," he said to a passing guard. "I'm new to town. Can you point me to the inn?"

"Aye." The guard gestured toward the far end of the market. "Closest one is Elsie's Flagon, down on the right. Look for the drunken barmaid."

Elijah nodded his thanks and continued along. Drunken barmaid? A sign hung on a building a little farther down. The artwork depicted a rather tipsy-looking woman holding a beer mug looked like she was in the process of falling over. Drunken barmaid, indeed.

Elijah went inside and wrinkled his nose. The market had smelled like any other small town, with the addition of animals and hay, but the tavern outright stank of old beer, food, body odor and what Elijah prayed wasn't puke.

"Have a seat," the older woman behind the counter called out to him. "I'll be there in a moment."

Nodding, Elijah found a table with a chair against a wall. He wasn't about to turn his back to the few people in here. None of them looked even remotely trustworthy.

The woman came to his table and looked him up and down. "New in town, aren't ye?"

"Is it that obvious?"

She smiled, revealing a smile missing a couple teeth. "You look like a scared rabbit. What can I get ye?"

Elijah had to think fast. "Um, ale, please?"

"No food?"

He started to shake his head but his stomach rumbled, vetoing that idea. "What's on the menu?"

"Roast pheasant and crusted bread."

"That'll work. Thanks."

She bustled off, leaving Elijah to casually take in his surroundings. Most of the patrons were busy with their own drinks and food, while a few chatted with one another. He amended his previous assessment about them, though. They all looked like farmers -- not scoundrels. The woman returned and set a wooden plate down, along with a battered metal mug and bent utensils.

"Six gold," she said.

Elijah discretely counted out seven coins and handed them to her. She smiled her thanks, tucked the extra one in her cleavage and went off to another table.

He tore off a piece of meat and tasted it. Not bad. Certainly better than he'd been expecting. He nibbled on it and the bread, while trying to avoid anyone's direct gaze.

When the barmaid returned to take his empty plate, he took a deep breath. "I'm new here," he said. "What can you tell me about this town?"

"Yer in Albronya, in the province of Tasmorum."

"Who is the lord here?" Elijah asked, not recognizing the town as one he'd been to in the game, though he did know of Tasmorum.

"Lord Jadir Alul." She studied him curiously. "Where are ye from?"

Elijah racked his brain for information from the character creation process. "Cosei," he said. "Biggest city in a land just to the south of Tasmorum."

Her eyes widened. "Oh! Do ye know of the Coseian Shadow?"

"Who?"

"Some say he's a spirit, others say he's just a man," she explained. "No one knows the truth or his full name, but folks call him Elian."

Elijah nearly choked on his ale. Well, that answered that question. "Um... I've heard of him, yes."

"He hails from Cosei, yes?"

Elijah nodded and managed to regain a bit of equilibrium. "Has he ventured here?"

"Oh, no. Though the guards know to watch for him."

"Do... do they know what he looks like?"

She grimaced. "I don't think so. I don't think anyone does except his lover."

Lover? He had a lover? "Who is this lover?"

She leaned down and whispered, her eyes light with mischief, "The captain of Cosei's guard."

Elijah barely stifled a whimper. That was part of Elian's storyline he had *not* reached in the game. Great. "Thanks for the information," he muttered.

"Sure thing. Can I get ye anything else?"

Elijah shook his head and waited until she was gone before burying his face in his palms. "What the hell?" he grumbled under his breath.

"You there."

Elijah lifted his head to meet a young man's gaze. "Yes?"

The man handed him a folded piece of paper. "I was told to find you and give you this."

"Find... me?" Elijah took the paper and opened it.

E -- *Meet me outside of Albronya.*
You are being tracked. We have to get you to safety.
Yours,
S

When Elijah glanced up, the young man had gone. Who was S? He tried to remember anyone from the beginning of the game, when he'd created the character of Elian Surgis, whose named started with S. No one came to mind. He'd left the city of Cosei rather early to explore.

Elijah left the inn and headed back toward the city gates. The letter said he was being tracked, which meant he had no idea who to trust or not. He kept his head down as he walked, making damn sure to not make eye contact -- especially with guards. He glanced up when he reached the city gate and his heart nearly stopped.

A faded poster nailed to one side of the gate drew a small group of curious onlookers. Elijah knew that particular hood and exactly what the face hidden by it looked like. The only distinguishing mark visible was the labyrinth tattoo just barely showing between the laces of the man's shirt. Elijah didn't dare look down to see if the same tattoo had suddenly appeared on his flesh. He didn't *want* to know.

He hurried out the gate and forced himself to walk away -- not run. When he got far enough away that he could no longer see the guards, he slipped into a cluster of trees. He rested his head back against a tree trunk and breathed in relief. A hand clamped down onto his mouth and his eyes flew open, a scream lodged in his throat.

Chapter Three

"Shh," a man whispered in his ear. "It's just me."
S.

Elijah waited while the man stepped in front of him. Holy fucking shit. This was Elian Surgis' lover? Elijah wanted to sink to his knees. *Now* he remembered. S stood for Sarin Eckhert, and the man was, indeed, the captain of Cosei's guard. Sarin was one of the first characters a new player meets upon starting the game. Insanely blue eyes set in a ruggedly handsome, square-jawed face stared at Elijah.

"You look like you've seen a ghost, love."

Elijah licked his lips when the hand left them. "Just… a long day."

Sarin smiled. "Aye." He stepped closer and Elijah breathed in the scents of leather and male. "Too long."

Before Elijah could answer, those kissable lips were on his, stealing what remained of his wits. He groaned and draped both arms around Sarin's neck and took everything the man offered. Hardness pressed against Elijah, drawing a slight shiver out of him. When Sarin pulled back, Elijah realized exactly why his character fell for the man. Storyline or no, Sarin Eckhert exuded rugged sex appeal.

"We need to get you somewhere safe," Sarin said. "King Mirov hired a well-armed, experienced tracker to hunt you down."

The king? Oh, fuck. Elijah never expected Elian's storyline to go that deep.

"Where are we going?" he asked.

Sarin hoisted a pack over one shoulder and readjusted the sword at his hip. "There's a post just beyond the border of Tasmorum. It was abandoned until a few months ago. The king sent a contingent there, but after the uprising, the men denounced the crown."

"So they're bandits," Elijah said.

Sarin shrugged. "In a sense, I suppose. But not like you seem to think. They were -- are -- honorable men. Unlike King Mirov."

"And they won't turn me over to him?"

Sarin cupped the back of Elijah's neck and rested their foreheads together. "I will never allow harm to come to you, Elian."

"Elijah."

Bluer-than-blue eyes narrowed. "What?"

"If I am on the run, if the king himself is after me, I need a new name," Elijah said.

"Then so be it," Sarin said with a nod. "Though forgive me if I slip in a moment of passion."

So not something Elijah needed to think about right now. Sarin smirked at him, apparently aware of exactly what went through Elijah's head.

"Believe me, love," Sarin said. "When we are safe, I will have you. It has been far too long since I touched you."

"Likewise," Elijah murmured.

Sarin kissed him once more and then released him. Elijah followed his lover into the woods, idly wondering if Sarin was a top or bottom. What would Elian do?

They continued on in silence for several minutes, Sarin leading the way deeper into the forest. Elijah couldn't tell which direction they were going, though it felt like they moved farther from the way he thought his cabin stood.

"What about the cabin?" he asked.

"I'll go back once you are safe and gather what I can," Sarin said. "Is there anything that would hint at your identity... or mine?"

Elijah had to think about that for a minute. "The books. I'm not sure which ones are there, though."

"Books?" Sarin stopped walking and turned. "Please tell me it's still hidden."

Elijah blinked. "What?"

"The Treatise. If Mirov gets his hands on that book, he will ransack the entire land of Timiria to find them."

Elijah wanted to ask who "them" was, but he didn't. "It's safe," he said. "I put it in one of the crates, beneath a false bottom."

Sarin nodded and started walking again. "Good. The last thing our Order needs is discovery that it still exists."

Elijah didn't know what the hell to make of that. One thing he did know: he needed to actually *read* that damn book.

Who -- or what -- was the Labyrinthine Cult? And why would the king of Timiria want to find them? The game's main plot line hinged on a fabled jewel -- not a group of people. Now, more than ever, Elijah wished he'd read some of the walk-throughs he'd found online. Maybe then he wouldn't be so ignorant about what the hell he'd just gotten himself into.

When they stopped once more, Sarin climbed up a hill and waved at Elijah to join him. A cave opened up in the side of the mountain. "We'll stay here for the night," Sarin said as he motioned for Elijah to follow.

"Is it empty?"

"It should be. The Order uses it as a waypoint, though no one's been here in quite some time."

They descended into the earth, and Elijah nearly

stumbled when Sarin conjured a fire from nothing. At Elijah's stunned look, Sarin smirked.

"I told you we don't forget our abilities -- even if we must keep them secret."

Abilities? Sarin Eckhert was a mage? Elijah shook off the questions bombarding his mind. If he asked, everything would unravel. He just had to play along like he knew what the hell was going on.

Sarin went down a narrow corridor that seemed to have been carved by hand from the rock. They emerged in a small room stocked with all manner of crates and barrels and a single bedroll. Sarin's ball of fire drifted to the ceiling and remained there, suspended as if it were a light fixture. Then he set his pack down and unbuckled his belt.

"We'll be safe here for the night," he said. "There's plenty of food in dry storage, and the Order sees to it that everything is well maintained for any of us needing shelter."

Sarin put his belt on one of the barrels, the sword resting atop it. Then he stepped closer to Elijah. Elijah let him remove the bow and quiver. Then the man undid the laces on Elijah's shirt. Elijah dared to glance down, a part of him unsurprised to see a labyrinth tattoo on his sternum.

"I remember when you got this," Sarin said, one slender finger tracing the pattern along Elijah's skin. "The others thought me insane."

"For?"

Sarin met Elijah's gaze. "For bringing you into the Order. You were the first outsider to ever become a Sentinel."

Elijah felt like he'd missed something very, very important. What the fuck was a Sentinel? He caught Sarin's hand and kissed the man's knuckles. "Have there been others since my joining?"

"No. The main group fractured when Mirov discovered one of our temples. Had you not left when you did, Mirov would have killed you, too."

Elijah didn't like the sound of that. "Too?"

What looked like sorrow passed over Sarin's handsome face. "Only a few of us escaped," he said. "Mirov went on a rampage, declaring all mages to be traitors. My position of guard captain has always kept my identity hidden."

"Can I ask you something?"

"Of course."

Elijah took a deep breath. "How are you here? As the captain of the guard, I can't imagine you would be allowed to just… disappear."

Sarin pulled away and turned. He went over to the bedroll and sat down. "I left on the pretense of finding you for Mirov. I had a small group of soldiers, but when I overheard one of them gossip about the tracker, I knew time was running out. I slipped free and gave the courier the note for you to meet me outside Albronya."

Elijah crouched in front of Sarin. "So now you're a fugitive as well." Sarin nodded. "Why would you risk everything like that?"

"I may be a mage," Sarin said, "but I also love you with every fiber of my being. Do you honestly think I would let them reach you first?"

Elijah opened his mouth to say… something. How did a guy respond to something like that? Instead of speaking, he pushed Sarin back and straddled the man, taking a kiss to shut them both up. Sarin grunted and slipped both hands under Elijah's shirt before tugging it off. Then he flipped them and ground their bodies together. Elijah grabbed Sarin's shoulders and rocked his hips upward, searching for more friction.

"Off," Sarin muttered as he shoved one hand between them to pull at the waistband of Elijah's pants. "I need to be inside you."

When Sarin rose up, Elijah kicked off his boots and managed to wiggle out of his pants. Sarin slid down Elijah's body, tongue blazing a trail from the hollow of Elijah's neck to his navel. Strong, slender fingers parted Elijah's thighs, and Sarin licked the dip where Elijah's hipbone met his pelvis. Elijah moaned and threaded his fingers through Sarin's long, pitch black hair. He guided Sarin lower until the man's tongue touched his cock.

Heat flowed over Elijah's flesh before enveloping him in the slick inferno of Sarin's mouth. Elijah shivered, hips lifting. Sarin held him down and sucked him to the root.

"Sarin!" Elijah grabbed the man's head and started fucking Sarin's mouth with quick strokes. "Oh, fuck... fuck..."

Sarin groaned and wet his fingers. Then he thrust both into Elijah's ass. Elijah bucked, spunk shooting down Sarin's throat. Sarin eased up and licked him clean, then slid back up Elijah's body.

"What in the names of the gods does 'fuck' mean?"

Elijah laughed, breathless but sated. "It means... 'that felt amazing,' at least under these circumstances." He met Sarin's gaze. "It has a lot of meanings, including use as a general curse. It also refers to the act of having sex."

"Ah." Sarin kissed him, and Elijah loved the taste of himself on Sarin's tongue. "Don't move," the man whispered.

Elijah nodded and Sarin got up. He rummaged

through the pack he'd set aside and returned. He knelt between Elijah's legs and pulled off his shirt. Elijah couldn't look away from the dark blue lines of *fur* that created dizzying patterns all over Sarin's skin. What the hell?

"What is it?" Sarin asked, hands working his pants open.

Elijah wasn't sure how to respond. Elian Surgis would have known such things about Sarin, right? "It's just been too long," he lied.

Sarin smiled and got rid of his pants and boots. Elijah swallowed at the sight that greeted him the moment Sarin's clothes were gone. Okay, Sarin Eckhert was not human -- not by *any* stretch of the imagination. More fur covered Sarin's body, from the waist down. Was he a shapeshifter? A werewolf?

Sarin opened a small vial and poured a thin line of clear liquid on his rather thick cock. Then he set the vial to the side and braced one hand by Elijah's head while the other stroked the length that would soon be buried inside Elijah's ass.

"You look nervous," Sarin chuckled. "It hasn't been that long, love."

Easy for you to say, Elijah thought. *You aren't two seconds from getting fucked by a huge cock attached to a canine-human hybrid.*

The more Elijah watched Sarin, the more he wanted that cock inside him. "Now," he said. He locked his legs around Sarin's waist and pinned the man against him. "Sarin, please…"

"As you wish."

Elijah's eyes rolled as Sarin eased inside. The burn and stretch stole Elijah's breath, and he gasped the second the head finally made it through the ring of muscle. Sarin groaned, head resting on Elijah's shoulder. The man's arms trembled as he held himself up off of Elijah.

Elijah would have encouraged him to keep going, to move, but words refused to come out. Pleasure mixed with the slight burn of his body getting used to Sarin's size. Elijah had never considered himself a size queen, but he had the distinct feeling Sarin had just spoiled him for all others.

"Love," Sarin murmured. "I have to move."

Elijah nodded. Sarin began rocking in and out, a little at a time. Then something changed. Elijah gasped as Sarin's cock swelled near the head, forming what felt like a knot. Every move Sarin made, the knot grazed Elijah's insides, rubbing his prostate.

"Oh, God... fuck... Sarin..."

Elijah clutched Sarin's shoulders, fingers digging into the man's skin. He'd never felt anything like it in his life. Sarin's strokes drove him up the fucking wall and back. The sensations built, growing stronger with every thrust. Sarin never quite pulled out, but sort of rocked into Elijah, over and over. Elijah's head swam as the pleasure built, centered in his ass. Sarin whispered something in another language and kissed Elijah.

Lights burst behind Elijah's closed eyes, and he screamed into Sarin's mouth. Intense heat flooded his body, and he swallowed every grunt and growl Sarin fed him. But it didn't stop. Sarin didn't go soft. Instead, he kept moving and kissed a path along Elijah's jaw. Elijah couldn't think, much less speak. He moaned when Sarin hit the sensitive spot just at the bend of his neck.

"*I ruqa aeui*," Sarin whispered.

Though Elijah had no clue what the hell Sarin just said, he made an educated guess. He nodded.

Exploring how he felt about a man he'd technically just met could come later. Much later. He wondered if Elian knew whatever language Sarin spoke.

Right now, it didn't matter. Sarin thrust into him again, and Elijah arched, his own cock hardening once more. He didn't care what Sarin was, so long as the man kept doing *that*.

Chapter Four

"It's time to go."

Elijah didn't want to go. He could have happily slept for another several hours, at least. Last night had been... something beyond amazing. He opened his eyes and found Sarin smiling at him. The man looked perfectly normal with clothes on -- not a single hint that, beneath the clothing, he sure as fuck wasn't human.

They packed up the few things they'd brought with them, and Sarin led the way out of the room and back into the cavern. Instead of going back the way they'd come, however, they went farther into the cave. Sarin conjured another flame and it floated above his outstretched palm, lighting their way. The ground began to incline and, before long, daylight broke the darkness. They emerged into a valley surrounded by towering mountains. A single wooden wall sat in the floor of the valley. Sarin started down the mountainside, Elijah following carefully.

When they reached a gate, guards merely nodded and opened it for them. Sarin walked in, and Elijah had no choice but to hurry after him before the gate closed.

The post looked fairly deserted, save for some of the guards along the walls. Several buildings stood around the edges, while a fenced off area sat near the center. Target dummies bore numerous marks. Out of one of the smaller buildings, an old man -- hunched over, with graying hair -- waved.

Sarin opened his arms wide and hurried over. "Rue!"

"I'd not thought to see you so soon," the old man

said. "Tell me, what brings you here?"

Sarin stepped aside and smiled at Elijah. "Him."

The old man looked Elijah up and down. Then he nodded. "A fine choice. He will make a grand Sentinel."

Sarin handed Elijah the pack he carried. "I'll return in two days," he said. "Ruelaeri is an old friend, and the rest of the men here can be trusted." He kissed Elijah. "Be safe, love."

"You, too," Elijah murmured.

Sarin waved goodbye and left through the gate. Elijah watched him go, then turned to Ruelaeri, who stared at him with a curious expression. Elijah cleared his throat and hefted the pack onto his shoulder.

"Follow me, young man," Ruelaeri said. "I have food and drink, and I'm sure you have questions."

Elijah went into the man's hut and his skin tingled. Whatever Ruelaeri was, Elijah had a feeling the man was far more powerful than many people thought. "So you know about the mages?"

"I will tell you everything you wish to know," the old man said. He extended a wrinkled hand to Elijah. "I am Ruelaeri, as you heard Sarin say."

Elijah shook the man's hand, surprised at the strength in the grip. "My name is Elijah."

"I have but one favor," Ruelaeri said, releasing Elijah's hand. "There is a black root that grows near the riverbed just outside the walls here."

"Let me guess… you want ten of them?"

Ruelaeri tilted his head. "How did you know? Are you an alchemist?"

Elijah snorted. "Lucky guess."

"Ah, I see." Ruelaeri sat at a battered wooden table in the center of the small hut. "Bring me the roots, and we will talk."

Elijah left the hut and headed toward the main gate. He'd barely known Sarin for a day, and he already missed the... man. It didn't matter what Sarin really was at this point. The mage had blown Elijah's mind the night before, and, if Elijah had any say about it, would do so again.

The guards at the post nodded and let Elijah out without a word. He found the river -- more like a wide stream, really -- and started searching for the distinctive black root along the bank. He found one fairly quickly and grabbed it. After a couple of good tugs, the thing came up out of the ground. Elijah brushed as much soil off of it as he could, then hunted for the other nine. By the time he'd found them all, the sun had begun to set. Elijah went back to the gate and the guards let him in.

Elijah went right for the old man's hut. Ruelaeri sat at the table, waiting patiently. "Here's your roots." Elijah handed Ruelaeri the plant parts the old man had requested. "Now will you tell me about the Labyrinthine Order?"

"The mages," the man said. "Yes, I can do that." He gestured for Elijah to shut the door of the hut. "They are the last followers of the goddess Laenasse. Some claim the men are cursed, doomed to hide from the world. Others say the mages are blessed by Laenasse herself."

"Are they all..." Elijah didn't know what to call it.

"Lupine?" Ruelaeri offered. "Yes. They represent Laenasse's totem animal: the wolf."

Elijah knew Sarin's true identity remained secret even from these people, so he had to word his next question carefully. "I once saw a man with furry designs on his torso. I know he's a mage of Laenasse.

Are the designs random?"

"Each mage's design is unique," Ruelaeri said. He smiled and parted the laces of his shirt to reveal blue designs, the same color as Sarin's. "They are marks of identity for us. Her colors are blue and silver, her symbols the wolf and the moon."

"You are one of them then," Elijah said. Ruelaeri nodded and closed the shirt once more. "Why is King Mirov after your Order?"

Ruelaeri spat. "Mirov," he snarled, sounding much like the wolf he and his mage brethren resembled. "The man is a coward. His chief advisor was exposed as a member of the Order. Mirov, like many others, fears magic. He had his advisor imprisoned and tortured for information. The advisor refused to divulge names and betray his fellow mages, so Mirov executed him."

Elijah swallowed. If Mirov was after the mages, then Sarin was in danger. "What about the Sentinels? Who are they?"

"Sentinels are the sworn protectors of the Order. Each Sentinel is connected to a mage, and they share our lupine qualities."

All but one, Elijah thought.

"You have more questions," Ruelaeri said. "I see them in your eyes."

"Have you ever experienced something that you knew wasn't rationally possible, yet... it happened?"

"A few times, yes." Ruelaeri leaned forward, arms on the wooden tabletop, hands folded. "Many things in Timiria are not what they seem to be, my young friend." His smile took on a knowing quality. "Do you truly believe you are the only 'traveler' we have had?"

Elijah blinked and sat back. "What are you

talking about?"

Ruelaeri gestured to Elijah with a nod of his head. "Your marking is not that of a Sentinel, as most would believe. It is the mark of someone not of our world. You are not the first to come here, and you will not be the last."

Elijah jumped up, knocking his chair backward onto the floor. "How do you know any of that?"

"I am the Seer of the Order," Ruelaeri answered, unmoved by Elijah's reaction. "It is my duty to know such things. We have had such people visit Timiria since the dawn of time."

Elijah fell against a wall and slid down to the floor. He wasn't the only person trapped here? How was any of this even possible? Would he ever get home? Swift on the heels of that thought came another: did he even *want* to return home?

Chapter Five

Commotion outside jerked Elijah out of a dead sleep. He crawled over to the wall and rose up enough to peer out of the one window in Ruelaeri's hut. A body landed on the dusty ground and blood pooled beneath the head. Elijah gasped and scrambled backward. Footsteps sounded outside the hut's door. A hand seized Elijah's shoulder and tugged him.

"Quiet," Ruelaeri whispered. "This way."

Elijah grabbed his pack and weapons and then followed Ruaelaeri to one corner of the hut. Ruelaeri murmured under his breath and the air shimmered, revealing a trap door in the floor. The mage opened it and gestured Elijah to go first.

"I will be right behind you," Ruelaeri whispered when Elijah hesitated. "The door will disappear once we are through it. Now go."

Elijah went down the wooden ladder and waited until Ruelaeri joined him. The trap door shut, dropping them into pitch dark. A ball of fire flared in Ruelaeri's palm, subdued but enough to light the narrow space in which they stood.

"Follow me," Ruelaeri said, "and watch your step. No one has used this tunnel in centuries, but I can't say the same for the wildlife."

"Great," Elijah muttered. Out of the frying pan and into, with his luck, a den full of mutant-size spiders or something.

The air in the passage turned cool the farther down they went. Water dripped from somewhere up ahead, and mushrooms sprouted from holes in the rock walls. Elijah sidestepped a rock, only to trip on a bone. He didn't dare look down, just kept going. If he didn't look, then he couldn't see the poor soul whose femur nearly made him face-plant onto the dirt and pebbles. The tunnel ended at a small cavern with two more openings branching off in different directions. One seemed relatively safe, while the other passage had been covered by thick white spider webs.

"Which way?" Elijah muttered. "Please don't tell me --"

"Here," Ruelaeri interrupted, heading straight for the web-encrusted hole.

Elijah groaned. "Figures." He readied his bow and an arrow, hoping he didn't have to use it. This was why he didn't like taking along followers or companions in games, especially in tight spaces. Friendly fire sucked.

Ruelaeri used the flame in his hand to burn away the webs, then he started down the passage. Grumbling, Elijah followed. Something moved a bit farther down -- something huge.

Elijah tapped Ruelaeri's shoulder. "Let me go first."

Ruelaeri flattened himself against one wall and Elijah squeezed past him. The hulking figure at the end rose up. Not a spider, but a wolf the size of a fucking horse. Just as Elijah nocked the arrow and drew, Ruelaeri grabbed the bow and pushed it downward.

"What the h --"

"Don't," the mage said. "He's one of ours."

Before Elijah could argue the wisdom of it, Ruelaeri hurried down the tunnel toward the wolf. Elijah rushed after him, ready to strangle the man. He skidded to a stop when the wolf's form shimmered and transformed into a human.

"Sarin!"

Sarin let out a sigh that sounded suspiciously like

relief. He grabbed Elijah's shoulders and dragged Elijah close for a kiss. "I feared the worst."

"How did you know?" Elijah asked.

"I spotted the king's soldiers as I headed back from your cabin."

"So Mirov knows then," Ruelaeri said. Sarin nodded. "They didn't see us leave, but I have no doubt they were searching for us."

Sarin sighed. "That little raiding party is nothing. Mirov has declared war on the Order. All Sentinels and mages are to be executed on sight."

"What?" Elijah stared at Sarin, then Ruelaeri. "No trial? No... anything?"

"He's the king," Ruelaeri said with a shrug. "In your world, perhaps things are different. But here in Timiria, the king holds absolute power until someone stronger dethrones him."

Elijah caught Sarin's confused expression. Shit. He had no idea how to explain that one.

"Son, there is much to discuss," Ruelaeri said, "but we must find the others."

Son? Sarin took Elijah's hand, offering no explanation of his own. "If we can make it to Ordul, we'll be ahead of the king's men. They seem to be going town by town, rooting out every suspicious person and searching for markings."

"Then let us be on our way," Ruelaeri said. "Come."

Elijah started to follow, but Sarin held him back. "What is it?"

"Why didn't you tell me?"

"Tell you... about what?"

Sarin nodded toward Elijah's chest and, no doubt, the tattoo that marked Elijah as a traveler -- not just a Sentinel.

Elijah sighed, glanced in the direction Ruelaeri had gone, then back to Sarin. "It's true. I don't know how to explain it in a way that will make much sense, though. I am from a country called America, and the year is 2013. This... place, Timiria, only exists as a world in a game called DungeonCrawl. I was playing that game when a storm hit and lightning shut down the power to my house. When I walked out my front door... I found myself here."

"I've heard of such people," Sarin said. "But I never thought I would meet one."

"What I can't figure out is how I -- well, how the character of Elian -- became your lover. I never encountered that in the game."

"I can explain that," Ruelaeri said from the tunnel he'd disappeared into a moment before. "These characters you play, they are real in this world. Timiria is real... to us. You -- and travelers like you -- wind up here and take on the identity of the characters they play in your world."

"So... it's like a form of possession," Elijah said. Ruelaeri nodded. Elijah blew out a breath. "I guess that makes sense. Sort of." He turned to Sarin. "Please don't think this changes anything."

Sarin smiled. "I don't. If you want, I can tell you how Elian and I met, and how we became lovers." He urged Elijah closer, voice lowering to a whisper meant for Elijah alone. "But you are right. It changes nothing between us."

Elijah licked his lips, heart racing. "Let's get somewhere safe. Then you can tell me anything you want. Just answer one question that's bugging me." Sarin cocked his head, as if waiting. "Who is Ruelaeri to you?"

"My father."

Chapter Six

The journey through the cave didn't take nearly as long as Elijah had expected. After an hour of walking, they emerged onto an outcropping of rock that overlooked a valley. A wide river rushed along the valley floor several hundred feet below the sheer drop. Ruelaeri took the lead once more and led them down a narrow path Elijah hadn't even seen. The path wound between boulders and bushes, trees and the mountainside. Every once in a while, Elijah spotted movement a bit farther, closer to the bottom of the valley.

A monolith towered over one section of the path, with two archways. The path led right under the monolith. As they passed beneath it, Elijah stopped for a moment to study the carvings along the walls and ceiling.

"Prayers to Laenasse," Ruelaeri said. "This is one of her ancient shrines."

"Are all her followers and worshippers like you and Sarin?"

"Oh, no. Sarin and I are her priests, but laypeople do not share the gift of lycanthropy."

Sarin gestured toward the other opening. "We are near Fort Ordul. There we will find food and rest."

Ruelaeri muttered something about pushy sons, and Elijah chuckled. The revelation that they were father and son hadn't been expected, especially given how Sarin called the old mage by the name of Rue. Looking at them now, though, Elijah saw tiny similarities here and there: the color of their eyes, the shape of their faces, the way Ruelaeri rolled his eyes and smirked when Sarin wasn't looking. They may be father and son, but the two men acted more like best friends. Elijah shoved away the acidic memories it brought up. The longer he spent in Timiria, living Elian Surgis' life, the more he wanted to stay forever.

At the bottom, a stone fortress loomed, rising out of the valley as if carved from the rock itself. Massive wooden gates opened for the three of them, while guards with swords and crossbows stood and watched.

People milled about the courtyard, many of them working. A few glanced up as Ruelaeri led the way toward what Elijah figured to be the main keep. A guard nodded in greeting and opened the door. Inside, warmth filled the air. Rich scents of food and drink mingled with smoke from countless pipes. Men and women sat at wooden tables along either side of the great hall, while children played on the floor with several dogs. The din quieted down, and a man at the far end stood and descended a set of steps.

"Ruelaeri, Sarin," he said. "I'm so pleased you are both safe. Come, come." He shook both of their hands. Then he faced Elijah. "Ah, so we finally meet the elusive Elian Surgis. You risk your life for us," the man said. "You have my thanks and the gratitude of my Order."

Not knowing what to do, Elijah erred on the side of caution and bowed. "It's my pleasure… my Lord?"

"Bah." The man grinned. "I am no one's lord. I merely do my best to keep the people here safe. I am Raig, warrior and unintentional head of Fort Ordul. Like Sarin, I am nothing more than a priest of Laenasse." He parted his shirt, revealing blue fur. "But enough of that. You must be hungry and tired. We have plenty of rooms at your disposal." He winked at Sarin. "Including a few with larger beds."

Sarin laughed. "Thank you, old friend."

Raig clapped his hands and several servants hurried over to them. He turned to Elijah, Sarin and Ruelaeri. "Please make yourself at home. When you have rested, I would much like to speak with all three of you."

"Thank you, Raig," Elijah said.

Elijah took a seat at one of the tables, and Sarin joined him. Ruelaeri wandered off to speak to another man. Sarin piled various bits of cheese, bread and meat onto two plates, then handed one to Elijah.

"Are all these people priests of Laenasse?" Elijah asked while they ate.

Sarin shook his head. "No. There are several Sentinels, and then there are the various workers who are sympathetic to our Order."

"Ruelaeri told me about Mirov's advisor and how Mirov executed him. Is the worship of Laenasse outlawed?"

"Not exactly," Sarin said in between bites. "While the worship itself is not against the king's laws, Mirov has declared all mages to be traitors to the crown."

"That's ridiculous!"

Sarin nodded. "There are many who readily agree." He finished eating and pushed the emptied plate away before sipping on his drink. "That said, there are those who side with Mirov. Namely due to fear of magic, I imagine, but it is enough to cause problems in towns where one would not expect any trouble."

Done eating, Elijah took a drink, realizing it was only water. "What do you mean?"

"Every town has a temple," Sarin explained, "and each temple has a healer. With the king on the warpath against all magic, the healers must be cautious. Even healing magic can lead to imprisonment if the wrong person were to witness it."

Elijah shuddered. "Makes me glad I'm not a mage."

Sarin smirked. "Oh, magic certainly has its uses, love."

One eyebrow raised, Elijah studied his lover. "Something tells me you aren't talking about things done in public."

Sarin winked at him. "You have experienced the lupine side of lovemaking with a priest of Laenasse." The mage stood and offered Elijah a hand. "Now come feel the magic we hold at our fingertips."

Elijah let Sarin pull him up. Then the mage drew him down a hallway until they reached a closed door. Sarin opened it and, once they were both inside, locked it behind them. Elijah looked around the room. For a fort, it wasn't too bad. The bed was bigger than he'd expected, plenty of room for the two of them. Sarin stepped up behind him, arms snaking around Elijah's waist.

"I feel like we are doing this for the first time," Sarin murmured in Elijah's right ear. "I suppose, in a sense, we are." He unlaced Elijah's pants and the cloth slipped to the floor. "Elian loved to take me."

Elijah groaned. "You just answered my prayers."

Sarin chuckled. "Good. Get undressed. I am craving this," he said, giving Elijah's hardening cock a firm squeeze.

The moment Sarin stepped back, Elijah finished stripping. The mage did the same, and Elijah stopped to look his fill. Sarin smiled and the sight of the mage's fingers wrapping around a thick cock nearly sent Elijah to his knees.

"Please tell me you have that vial of slick stuff."

Sarin released himself and retrieved the vial from a pack beside his own clothing. He handed Elijah the vial and stretched out on the bed. Elijah set the vial to the side, then knelt on the bed between Sarin's legs. Fur caressed his thighs when Sarin's legs moved, and the mage's cock leaked beads of opaque precome onto a furred belly.

"Where I come from," Elijah said, stroking one hand along the blue fur on Sarin's inner left thigh, "there are people who would give anything to get their hands on you. We call them furries."

Sarin laughed. "And you?"

Elijah didn't answer. He just bent and licked Sarin's cock from base to tip. The mage gasped and grabbed Elijah's head, urging him to keep going. Elijah sucked the head into his mouth and hummed. Sarin moaned his name, hips lifting and falling.

Elijah somehow managed to get two fingers slick and rubbed them over Sarin's hole. Sarin growled low as both fingers sank deep inside. Elijah wondered if Sarin had the same inner anatomy. He angled his fingers and found a familiar spot. Sarin shouted, his entire body jerking. Elijah chuckled, the sound muffled by the mage's cock. He stroked Sarin faster, sucked harder.

"Please," Sarin panted. "Now. Take me!"

Unable to resist, Elijah pulled off of Sarin's cock and got his own slick. He withdrew his fingers and pushed his cock in their place. Sarin's eyes rolled back and the man's legs locked around Elijah's waist, tugging him forward. Elijah buried himself to the balls and they both groaned.

"Fuck, you're unbelievable," Elijah muttered, forehead resting on Sarin's.

"Just wait." Sarin rolled his hips. "How do you say it? Fuck me?"

"Keep that up, and I'll come."

Elijah kissed Sarin to quiet the mage's chuckle. Every thrust and rock drove him in and out of out of the finest ass he'd ever known. He found Sarin's hands and linked their fingers. Pressing the man's hands on the bed, Elijah sped up.

Heat rushed through him like a flash fire, and electricity buzzed along every nerve. Elijah gasped, his movements stuttering for a moment.

"Don't stop," Sarin whispered.

Elijah had no intention of stopping. Spurred on by the magic sizzling across his skin, he kissed Sarin hard and rolled them. On top, Sarin sat up and, head back, ground down onto Elijah over and over. Elijah ran both hands up the mage's torso, fingers tracing each furry design. Sarin rocked faster.

"More," Sarin gasped. He grabbed Elijah's hands and drew them up to where the patterns began near his nipples.

Elijah let his fingers follow each swirl, each curve. Sarin let out a low, feral groan. Whatever the designs were, they apparently served as erogenous zones. Elijah pressed harder and began petting the furred designs.

"Yes!"

Sarin jerked and come splattered onto Elijah's chest. The mage's ass clamped tight around Elijah's cock. Elijah shouted, hands flying to Sarin's hips to pin the man down. Pleasure coiled deep in Elijah, and he slammed into Sarin as he came.

Dizziness set in fast. Sarin leaned down and kissed him softly. Elijah wanted nothing more than to curl up with the mage and sleep. He'd never felt so drained.

"What did you do?" he murmured as Sarin moved off of him.

Sarin chuckled and wiped them both clean before coaxing Elijah to get under the blanket. "In your world, I believe it is called sex magic."

Chapter Seven

They met Ruelaeri and Raig in another part of the keep, far away from the others still milling about in the great hall. Elijah stopped in the doorway, his jaw hitting the floor in utter shock. When he'd last seen Ruelaeri, the man had been old, wrinkled. This Ruelaeri looked a lot younger -- still old enough to be Sarin's father, but not nearly as old as he'd seemed.

"Ah, there you are," Ruelaeri said. He got up from where he'd been sitting at a table.

Elijah felt as dumbfounded as he probably looked.

Ruelaeri chuckled. "Do you really think me as feeble as I appeared before? We mages have many abilities at our disposal, glamor among them. If I present myself as an old man, who in their right mind would think me a powerful mage?"

"You have a point," Elijah said. "So is this your true appearance?"

"Yes, though, like Sarin, I can take a wolf form." Ruelaeri gestured for them to sit at the table.

Raig waited until they were all seated before speaking. "Rue has told me of how you came to us," he said, his gaze settling on Elijah. "We have had others pass through who are like you."

"Are any of them still here?"

Raig shook his head. "From my experience, they seem to prefer wandering on their own. In this world, I surely wouldn't, but I can't make them stay -- even if it's for their own protection."

Elijah couldn't blame them, though he figured the travelers' minds would promptly change they knew what sort of troubles plagued Timiria.

"The last of the Order arrived overnight," Ruelaeri said. "How are our defenses here?"

Raig grimaced. "Laughable. Fort Ordul can weather a small raiding party, but anything more will be a problem. There are still parts needing repairs."

"How long have you all been here?" Elijah asked him.

"Four months. The fort was abandoned but greatly damaged from Timiria's last war. It took us two months just to clear out all the bodies."

Elijah groaned and thanked every god imaginable he hadn't been here for that task.

"What do we need to finish the repairs?" Sarin asked. "And how much time will it take?"

"More time and resources than we have." Raig sighed and leaned forward, arms braced on the table top. "Sentinel scouts reported a large force marching this way. We can't hold this place against it."

"Are you suggesting we leave?" Sarin asked. "Where would we go?"

Ruelaeri leaned closer, his voice lowering to a whisper. "There is a cave system nearby, unused by all except for the occasional bandit. The entrance is not far from here, and, unless I am mistaken, there is a hidden entrance to the tunnel leading to it down in the jail."

"We need someone to clear out the bandits," Raig said. "A group of them set up camp down there, near the end of the tunnel. They're led by a surly orc named Gorgc. They won't leave, and I won't risk our people until they are gone."

Elijah felt all three gazes land on him at once. "How did I know I'd be the one?" He sighed. "All right, show me how to get there."

"We can spare a few men, but --"

"No," Elijah interrupted Raig. "Trust me. It'll be

a lot easier if I don't have to worry about someone else getting hurt or in the way."

Sarin gripped his arm. "Love…"

"Sarin, I'll be fine." Elijah kissed the mage softly. "I promise."

Sarin nodded. "Be careful."

"I will."

Raig got up, and Elijah followed the man out the door. They stopped at Elijah and Sarin's room long enough for Elijah to grab his bow, quiver and daggers. Then they headed down a long hallway to another wooden door, this one banded in rusting iron. Raig pulled out a key and unlocked the door. Then he handed Elijah another key. "This will unlock the door at the far end of the jail corridor. The tunnel isn't very long and will lead you right to the cave where Gorgc and his bandits are camped."

"Okay. Any tips?"

"Orcs hit hard," Raig said. "The other bandits are humans, but if they catch you unaware, you'll be dead before you take your next step. Best tactic is to pick them off from a distance before engaging Gorgc."

Elijah nodded. "Got it."

"Good luck, and come back to us in one piece."

Elijah went through the door and waited until Raig locked it. Once his eyes adjusted to the dim light from a few torches along the walls, he slipped his bow off his shoulder. He peered through the bars of each jail cell, thankful that there were no skeletons waiting for him. In his gaming experience, places like this were inevitably filled with skeletons, ghosts, rogue mages and bandits. When he reached the door at the far end, he unlocked it and pocketed the key. He took a deep breath, then stepped into the darkness of the tunnel.

The tunnel, he discovered, wasn't quite as long

as he'd expected. He soon found himself standing on a narrow ledge that circled the top half of an open cavern. Below, he counted six bandits sitting around a fire. A seventh stood at a wooden table, hulking over the furniture and as green-skinned as any orc in a video game. The only way up to the ledge where Elijah crouched was a narrow ramp of wooden boards.

Elijah took a deep, quiet breath. He drew an arrow and nocked it. Doing this in a game was easy. Doing it in real life, with no healing potions a button press away, was definitely not on the simple list. He aimed for one of the guards, but just before he readied himself to fire, he spotted a tripwire at the foot of the ramp. He glanced up and grinned. Huge rocks hung in a rope net over the cavern floor -- close enough to land on at least two of the bandits near the fire. Elijah said a silent prayer, then fired.

Rocks pummeled the cavern floor, kicking up a cloud of dust and dirt, and sounding like a thunderstorm. Elijah nocked another arrow and waited until the dust began to clear before taking another shot. Three bandits lay dead beneath the stone, and the fourth landed over one of the rocks, an arrow in his chest. The remaining two, looking battered but alive, circled the area, swords drawn. Gorgc snarled and scanned the cavern.

"*Shav availkord, davulk!*" the orc shouted.

Elijah had no clue what the hell the creature said. He readied another arrow and brought down one of the two bandits flanking Gorgc. The other bandit and the leader both spun around.

Gorgc grabbed the last bandit's shirt and jerked the man close. "*Karr han!*" He threw the bandit to the ground.

The bandit scrambled up and started for the

ramp. Elijah shot him in the head, and the body tumbled back down to land at Gorgc's booted feet. The orc kicked the corpse and growled.

"Ukorokk daark. I varr karr avai navkord!"

Elijah fired and the arrow slammed into Gorgc's biceps. The damn orc growled, broke off the shaft and continued. Hands beginning to shake, Elijah took another shot. This one halted the bandit leader for a moment when it buried in his torso. He snapped it and tossed it aside. Then he peered into the dark and those black eyes widened.

"Tholo avai ulo, vhork!"

Gorgc lifted his massive sword and swung. Elijah ducked and rolled, and the sword came down onto the ground where his body had been. Gorgc roared and charged him. Elijah tossed his bow aside and drew his dagger. The bandit leader crashed into him, sending them both into the cave wall. Elijah retched at the putrid stench of the orc's breath. Gorgc seized Elijah's throat and lifted him, grinning to reveal broken rows of rotten teeth.

The world began to gray at the edges. Elijah couldn't swallow around the orc's hand on his neck. He raised his dagger and prayed he could focus long enough. He plunged the blade into the orc's left eye.

Gorgc howled and released him. The orc stumbled backward, clutching his bleeding face. Elijah gasped and sucked in several quick breaths. He rushed Gorgc and shoved his dagger under the orc's chin, right into the creature's throat. He jumped away, and the hulking body collapsed onto the ground with a final grunt.

Elijah grabbed his bow and staggered back down the tunnel, toward the jail. When he reached the door Raig had locked, he pounded on it. The door opened a moment later, and Elijah collapsed into someone's waiting arms.

"Thank the gods."

"Sarin?"

"Shh…" Sarin helped him away from the door. "You're safe now."

"How did you… Why are you down here?"

"The king's soldiers are on the move," Sarin said. "We've gathered everyone and have been waiting for you to return."

"Bandits are dead," Elijah muttered.

"Let us pray we don't have anything else to contend with." Raig helped Sarin get Elijah upright once more. "Are you all right?"

"Yeah, just…" Elijah rubbed his neck. "You weren't kidding about orcs."

"Why do you think some of us mages wear metal armor?"

Elijah nodded. "Can't blame you there."

"We need to get the others into the caves," Ruelaeri said, coming up behind Raig.

Shouting sounded from somewhere outside. It spurred all four of them into movement. Ruelaeri and Raig ran down the corridor to gather the people, while Elijah helped Sarin get both doors open and ready. People -- men, women, children -- and dogs flooded the jail. Elijah ushered them all through the last door. Then he nodded to Sarin and took the lead to guide them all through the caves.

Chapter Eight

The group made it past the bandits without trouble. Elijah heard several groans and a few whimpers -- namely from the kids -- but he kept them moving. When the cave narrowed again, he readied his bow. He gestured for the others to wait while he scouted ahead. He stopped when the tunnel turned left. As he edged his way around the bend, he sensed someone behind him.

Elijah made it far enough to peer into the open cavern beyond the tunnel. No fires or people, but that didn't mean it was safe. He gestured for Sarin to hang back before he approached the end of the tunnel. Movement to the right of the exit startled him, and he shrank back, heart pounding.

This wasn't a game anymore. Spiders that size weren't supposed to exist.

"Big," he whispered. "Huge fucking spiders."

Sarin snorted softly. "Welcome to Timiria."

Elijah groaned low. "I only saw one to the right, but that doesn't mean it's alone."

Sarin nodded. "Let me go in first." Elijah glared at him, but Sarin held up a hand. Fire swirled on his palm. "Trust me."

Despite his misgivings, Elijah let Sarin ahead of him. The mage, fire in hand, worked around the bend and toward the opening. An odd chittering filled the cavern and pebbles rattled when something big moved. The fire in Sarin's hand flared.

The noise grew louder and an enormous shape blocked the tunnel. Flames shot out from Sarin's hand, and the monstrous spider actually screeched. It scrambled backward, then rose up, fangs dripping with venom, front legs poised for attack.

Elijah never shot an arrow so fast in his fucking life. It hit the spider's abdomen, and the creature let out another wicked scream. The thing retreated and Sarin advanced on it. The mage burned the spider until it stopped twitching.

Motion from the left was the only warning they had. Another spider leapt onto Sarin and pinned him to the ground. Sarin grabbed its fangs and moved as the spider tried to stab him.

"Sarin!"

Elijah fired another arrow. The spider shrieked and left Sarin to come after Elijah. Sarin got up and roasted it from behind as Elijah put another arrow into the thing's head. The spider crumpled, legs curled.

Elijah hurried to Sarin. "Are you okay?"

"Yes." Sarin shivered. "I think that's as close to a spider as I wish to ever be."

"No kidding." Elijah looked around. "I think those were the only ones," he said, scanning the web-covered cavern for any more moving shapes.

"I believe so. We need to get the others through here quickly. I don't know how long my father's magic will conceal the door in the jail."

"Right." Elijah patted Sarin's shoulder and took a quick kiss. "Get the rest. I'll make sure everything's clear."

Elijah grabbed one of the spider's legs and winced. "Gross," he muttered as he tugged the corpse out of the way. "Ugh!" He wiped his hand on his pants, only to realize he still had bandit blood on them. "Oh, God. I so need a shower."

"Hurry," Sarin said. He stepped through the opening and motioned for the people to come into the cavern.

"This way." Elijah took the lead again and led them all to the far side. A ledge hung over the ground by several feet. "We can camp here for the night. Sarin, can you get a fire going?"

Sarin started stacking bits of wood and dried leaves onto a small pile of rocks. Then he conjured more fire in his hand and blew on it. The leaves and wood caught, and the flames instantly warmed the cavern. Ruelaeri and Raig helped some of the others with food preparation.

"I want to check out the other tunnel," Elijah said, nodding toward the only other opening. "If it's clear, is there a way we can block the one leading back into the caves?"

"It won't be quiet, but we can." Sarin glanced at him. "You need to eat."

"I think I'm too rattled, to be honest."

Sarin took Elijah's hands and wet them with water from a jug one of the women had brought. He handed Elijah a scrap of cloth to dry off and then pulled Elijah to one side. "Sit." When Elijah did, Sarin knelt and closed his eyes. He ran both hands over Elijah's body, from head to toe. Tingling followed, like some bizarre shield formed around Elijah.

"What are you doing?"

"Easing my mind," Sarin said. He stopped and cupped Elijah's face. Those blue eyes took Elijah's breath away. "Reassuring myself you are unharmed."

"I'm okay, Sarin." Elijah leaned closer, but stopped. "Question. How are guys like us treated here?"

"The same as anyone else," Sarin answered. "Why?"

Elijah rested his forehead to Sarin's and sighed. "In my world, it depends on where you are. Things are getting better, but we're still vilified."

Sarin leaned against the cave wall and held out a hand. Elijah joined him, content to snuggle close. "You're the first traveler I've met. What is your life like there?"

Elijah shuddered. He honestly didn't want to even think about it. "You want the truth?" He felt Sarin nod. "Awful. My parents were the type who despised people like us. When they found out I liked guys, they threw me out. Because my dad is a big-time politician, though, they wanted me to stay out of sight. They shoved me into a house they owned, paid all my bills. I had to keep quiet and hidden."

"That's a horrible thing to do to your child," Sarin grumbled.

"What about you and Ruelaeri?"

"What could he say?" Sarin shrugged. "He and Raig have been lovers for longer than I've been alive."

Elijah sat up and stared at the mage. "You're kidding."

"Not at all. My mother died minutes after I was born. Rue raised me."

"So… how did your mother feel about your dad and Raig?"

"She didn't care. She was an old friend of my father's, and she wanted a child. He offered to help her. Raig gave them his blessing, and my father slept with my mother."

"Wow. That's… a hell of a friendship," Elijah said.

Sarin smiled. "Always has been."

"I'm sorry about your mom, though."

"It's fine. I never knew her, so I honestly can't say if I miss her or not." Sarin glanced over to the group, where Raig and Ruelaeri now sat together, talking and smiling with one another. "But it would kill me to see anything happen to Raig or Rue."

"Why do you call him Rue? I would think you'd call him... Dad or Father."

"Habit, I think," Sarin said. "We can't be so open around people we don't know. Rue is the Seer of the Order -- one of the oldest still living, and one of the most important. He acts as our historian as well. If something were to happen to him, our history would be lost."

"Did he write the Treatise?"

"Yes."

"I remember, while playing the game, that Elian stole it from a lord's home. How did the lord get it?"

"He stole it from us," Sarin said. "You -- well, Elian Surgis -- simply returned the favor." Sarin pulled Elijah back to him and kissed the top of Elijah's head. "Can I ask you something?"

"Sure."

Several moments passed and Elijah wondered if Sarin would continue.

"Some travelers have returned to their lives, while others have found ways to switch back and forth at will."

Elijah had the feeling he knew where this was going. Taking advantage of everyone being occupied, he straddled Sarin's lap and slipped his fingers through the mage's hair, tilting Sarin's head until those blue eyes met his. "I hated -- hated -- my life. I couldn't be who I wanted to be, and before I got zapped here, a message from my father made it very clear how much they despised me." He leaned down and kissed Sarin softly, whispering, "I don't *want* to return."

Sarin groaned and gripped Elijah's hips, pinning Elijah down onto him. "What I wouldn't give to have you alone right now."

"Likewise," Elijah murmured. He grinned and worked a hand between them. When he cupped Sarin's cock, the mage gasped. "How quiet can you be?"

"You can't be serious."

Elijah managed to get Sarin's pants unlaced and wrapped his fingers around his lover's thick cock. "Shh…" he whispered as he began stroking.

"Love…" Sarin breathed. "Faster."

Elijah sped up the rhythm and kissed Sarin, swallowing the man's soft moans. The thighs beneath Elijah tightened, and Sarin's fingers dug into Elijah's hips. The mage thrust into Elijah's fist, over and over. Elijah rubbed his thumb along the slit and Sarin bucked. Heat poured over Elijah's fingers as the mage's groan filled Elijah's mouth. Elijah broke the kiss and brought his hand up to lick it clean.

"Keep that up, and I'm hunting for an empty cave," Sarin growled.

Elijah chuckled. "Wouldn't hear me complain."

* * *

Being underground threw Elijah's internal clock for a loop. He rubbed his eyes and looked around. Others were beginning to wake up, though Sarin still slept beside him. Elijah leaned down and kissed Sarin's head.

"Time to get moving, babe."

Sarin grumbled something unintelligible, but he rolled over and blinked up at Elijah a moment later. "Any idea what time it is?"

"Not a clue," Elijah said. "I'm not exactly used to sleeping in caves."

It took several minutes, but eventually everybody was up and ready to move. Elijah studied the entrance they'd come through the night before.

"We need to block it somehow," he said.

"That can be done." Ruelaeri gestured for everyone to back up. Then he raised his hands and began chanting. "*Eorsr omd ksuma, raad kae corr. Ikvada uir amakeak.*"

The cave shook and dust fell from the ceiling. Several people gasped and backed up even more. Elijah watched, spellbound, small rocks began falling from above. He urged everyone farther away. Ruelaeri joined them.

Small rocks and pebbles gave way to larger ones. Several people covered their ears and they all watched as the rocks piled up in the entrance, completely blocking it. Ruelaeri nodded.

"Wow..." Elijah muttered.

"That should give us some time," Ruelaeri said. "Shall we?"

Elijah took the lead once more and led the group through the other tunnel. Bow drawn, he took his time, determined not to lead them into any trouble. Before long, he spotted daylight. The tunnel ended near a waterfall. Elijah breathed in the fresh air. Everyone left the cave, doing much the same thing. Several of them patted him on the back in thanks for getting them through unscathed.

The small valley looked rather well protected. Rock walls towered on all sides, with only a narrow opening that led out into the wilderness. The waterfall poured out from the mountain, creating a deep pool of clear blue water. Elijah crouched along the side and washed off his hands and face. A shadow appeared beside him.

"Feels good to be out of those damn caves," Sarin said as he sat down. He tugged off his boots, pulled up his pants legs, and dangled his feet in the water. "I'll be glad when we can stop running."

"Where are we going, anyway?" Elijah did the same thing and sighed when the cool water soothed the aches he didn't realize he'd had.

"Here," Ruelaeri said from behind them. He handed Elijah a map. "The stronghold of Pelarum is our safest bet. It is run by a lord sympathetic to the Order, who bears no love for Mirov. We can rest there. It is safe and well-defended."

Elijah studied the map while Sarin looked on. "How much farther?"

"At best guess, another day's travel," Ruelaeri said. "Provided we don't run into trouble."

"All right." Elijah rolled up the map and handed it back to Ruelaeri. "Then that's where we go. For now, we can let the people rest here. I think we're safe enough."

Ruelaeri nodded and wandered off. Elijah caught Sarin smiling.

"What?"

"You may not have meant to come to Timiria, but you fit well here."

As Elijah gazed at the group of people now laughing and bathing, kids playing with the dogs, he realized just how right it felt.

"I'm finally somewhere I belong," he said, "as strange as that may sound."

Sarin wrapped one arm around Elijah's shoulders. "It doesn't sound strange. Timiria might be rife with troubles you are not accustomed to, but it has its charms."

Elijah couldn't agree more. He wondered, briefly, about what would happen back in his world. His parents would no doubt think he'd gone and died of some disease or something equally controversial to their sensibilities. Here, though, he didn't have to worry about hiding who he was, and he finally had someone he could call his own.

"Other travelers may want to leave," he said, "but I'm staying."

Patch Day (DungeonCrawl 2)

Mychael Black

PvP takes on a whole new meaning when Elijah Burrows meets a fellow gamer in Timiria.

Gamer Elijah Burrows has rather seamlessly taken over the life of his game character, Elian Surgis, in the world of Timiria. Alongside his lover, the lupine mage Sarin Eckhert, Elijah leads survivors of Sarin's mystical order through the wilds of the province of Tasmorum. They manage to stay just one step ahead of Timiria's monarch, King Mirov, who seeks to destroy every magic-wielding soul connected to the Labyrinthine Order.

From encounters with a mysterious group of traders on the road, to a revelation of epic proportions, it's a miracle Elijah has any time to explore his relationship with Sarin. Then Fate throws a wrench into the mix: the appearance of another "traveler" -- another gamer stuck in the game world Elijah now calls home. But this particular gamer has ulterior motives that have nothing to do with the Order's survival.

Chapter One

To say Timiria was unlike Earth would be the understatement of the century. While Timiria had vast swaths of forests, lakes that could swallow a small Earth city, and more mountains than Elijah Burrows had ever seen in his life; it also boasted races such as elves and orcs, and probably dwarves. Elijah had already encountered more giant eight-legged wildlife than he ever cared to see, and he had the feeling things only got bigger elsewhere. When he'd first found himself stuck in this dangerous yet beautiful game world, his initial thought had been to find a way back home. Now, the more time he spent in Timiria, the less he wanted to return to his little hell on Earth.

He sat near the fire and nibbled on a piece of perfectly-cooked rabbit. Food was another thing he'd had to get used to here. Timiria's larger towns and cities had shops that sold food, not to mention a plethora of taverns, but out here in the wild, Elijah had to put his old archery skills to good, practical use. Though, he had to admit, fresh, fire-roasted rabbit tasted a hell of a lot better than boxed macaroni and cheese.

Across the campsite, a group of men talked in hushed tones. Elijah couldn't make out what they said, but he really didn't care. He watched the forest around and beyond them, more alert than he ever had been. One of those men was his -- well, his game character's -- lover. Elijah still hadn't quite wrapped his head around the notion that this world and the people in it actually existed outside the game itself. From what he'd gathered, he had essentially taken over the life of Elian Surgis, the thief he'd created to play the game

DungeonCrawl. He certainly never got to the point in Elian's story line that involved a lover.

The group broke up and a tall figure walked around the fire, toward Elijah. Sarin Eckhert -- and his fellow mages of the Labyrinthine Order -- were lupine creatures. They looked human until they undressed. Even now, beneath the parted front of Sarin's white shirt, Elijah spotted swirls of blue fur.

The mage lay on the ground, head on Elijah's thighs. Unnaturally blue eyes gazed up at Elijah. "You look pensive," Sarin said.

Elijah fed his lover a piece of rabbit. "Just reflecting on everything, I guess. I still haven't quite gotten used to being here, in this world. To me, it was nothing but a game -- a good escape from a lonely life -- but still a game."

Sarin chewed for a moment, his expression thoughtful. "Do you still want to find a way back home?" he asked finally.

Elijah glanced up at the people he'd helped escort out of a ruined fort when soldiers had come to kill every last soul on the king's orders. He didn't know many of them, save for Sarin, Sarin's father Rue, and Rue's lover Raig; but he'd come to think of them as his personal responsibility. As his family.

"I don't think so," he admitted. "The longer I'm here, the more it feels like home."

A tug on his shirt drew him down to meet Sarin's lips. The mage sighed and scrambled Elijah's brain without even trying. No wonder Elian Surgis had fallen in love with Sarin. Even though Elijah hadn't known Sarin long at all -- just a few days -- he found himself slowly following in Elian's footsteps. Elijah knew Sarin loved him -- well, Elian -- but he also knew Sarin understood the weird circumstances behind why

Elijah had yet to return the sentiment whenever Sarin mentioned love. Motion nearby broke the spell between them. Elijah looked up to find the campers settling in for the night.

"I'll take first watch," Elijah said when Raig, the unofficial leader of their merry little group, approached.

"Are you certain?"

Elijah nodded. "Yeah." He waited until Sarin sat up and then he grabbed his bow and quiver. "I'll yell if there's trouble."

"I'll sit with you," Sarin said.

"I'll come relieve you both in four hours." Raig ducked into the makeshift tent he shared with Rue.

Elijah led the way to a small outcropping of rocks that marked the outer boundary of the clearing in which they'd camped. The sides were surrounded by a small expanse of trees, but then the canyon walls towered over everything else. A waterfall tumbled from an opening high up and spilled into a pool where he and the others had bathed and relaxed earlier. The only opening was a narrow pass about the width of four men. The little valley provided a bit of shelter from the chilly night winds and the possibility of bandits. The rock walls were too jagged and steep for anyone to climb.

Elijah sat down, and Sarin settled behind him. The mage pulled Elijah back against a solid, muscular body. Sarin wasn't like any mage Elijah had ever imagined. The man was physically strong and incredibly agile. He, along with his fellow mages, preferred chainmail armor as opposed to cloth. Elijah relaxed, bow within easy reach.

"I promised to tell you how Elian and I became lovers."

Elijah nodded. "Something tells me it had to do with Elian's profession as a thief."

Sarin chuckled. "You could say that. The first time we met, I'd been the one to capture him. He hadn't been a thief very long -- only a few months -- and his skills had yet to grow. At the time, I wasn't the Captain. I was just a guard tasked with leading a group to apprehend him. But..." Elijah felt Sarin shake his head. "When I first saw Elian, all I wanted was to kiss him. I didn't get that kiss until two days after we put him in jail."

"What happened then?"

"I made excuses to look in on him," Sarin said. "When I finally realized I couldn't deny the desire, I freed him. He kissed me before slipping into the tunnel we used for prisoners."

Elijah smiled. "How did you become lovers?"

"He returned," Sarin said. "I became Captain a few months after. The Lord of Cosei believed Elian to be dead. I convinced everyone he had died in the night and I'd disposed of his body. Shortly after my promotion, I received an unsigned letter from a courier, telling me to find a cabin tucked into the woods north of Cosei. When I arrived alone, Elian was there, waiting for me. That was the first night we slept together, six years ago."

"Wow. How did the others react when they realized Elian wasn't dead?"

"Have you heard anyone mention the Coseian Shadow?"

Elijah nodded.

"Well, the Coseian Shadow is supposedly Elian Surgis' ghost."

Elijah snorted. "So I'm a spirit now?"

"In a sense, yes. Though I think there are those

who believe you to be flesh and blood, resurrected with magic."

"That explains the wanted posters," Elijah muttered.

They fell into a companionable silence for several minutes. Elijah rested his head back against Sarin's shoulder and gazed out at the forest sprawling before them. They had a day's travel until they reached Pelarum, a stronghold ruled by a lord sympathetic to the Labyrinthine Order and who, according to Rue, bore no love for King Mirov.

"Rue said we're heading to a stronghold called Pelarum. Have you ever been there?"

"Once," Sarin answered. "It's been a few years, but Lord Aven despises the king and he has been a friend of the Order for quite some time."

"Anything I should know before we get there?"

"No one outside the Order knows Rue is my father," Sarin said. "While, as a whole, we trust Aven, we can't say the same for everyone in his keep."

"Understood. What can we expect on the way there?"

"It's not unusual to run into the occasional merchant wagon or small caravan," Sarin explained. "And there are bandits, though they tend to take up posts in caverns and ruined towers. If we stay clear of such places, we should be fine."

"What happens if we encounter any of the king's men?"

Sarin sighed. "We get the others to safety. Only the priests of Laenasse possess magic, and not all of us are accustomed to battle. If we can avoid conflict, it will be best."

Elijah nodded, though he had the distinct feeling that would be easier said than done.

Chapter Two

The night went by without much incident. Raig and Rue came to relieve Sarin and Elijah after four hours. Elijah would have happily dragged Sarin into their makeshift tent for a bit of fun, but after all the excitement of escaping Fort Ordul, the only thing either of them wanted was sleep.

Someone nudged Elijah and he grumbled. "Morning already?"

"Afraid so," Raig said.

"What time is it?" Elijah peered up from where he'd been snuggled against Sarin, his face buried in the mage's pitch black hair. The sun wasn't quite up yet.

"We have maybe an hour or so before sunrise. It's best we get moving now," Raig answered. "I'm going to get the others roused."

Elijah sighed and nodded. He kissed Sarin's head and sat up. Raig went around each little part of the camp, waking the rest of their caravan-type group. Women and men then woke the children, who seemed even less enthusiastic than Elijah about the notion of getting up. Elijah bent and brushed black hair from an enticingly handsome face. He was only slightly surprised to meet Sarin's gaze.

"I'll be happy when we get to Pelarum," Sarin muttered.

"You and me both."

Elijah began packing their things into the bag Sarin handed him. When everyone else was ready, Rue passed out a few pieces of crusty bread and Raig filled battered metal cups with water. Elijah nibbled on his breakfast and watched while the women bathed the kids at the pool's edge. Rue wandered over, map in hand. He sat beside Elijah and Sarin.

"We have two options for reaching Pelarum," Rue said. He opened the map and spread it out on the ground. He traced one route with a fingertip. "This way is the quickest, but it's open. We may encounter a merchant or two, perhaps farmers as well, but bandits are also a possibility." His finger moved to another, more curving line. "This route takes us through the Olven Foothills. They run along the base of the Ethur Mountains. A bit more rugged and more time-consuming, but safer."

Elijah studied the two roads on the map. "Is there a way to switch once we go one way or another?"

"Here." Rue pointed to a small space that seemed to go over what looked like a river. "The town of Borova serves as a crossroads between the two routes. Mostly farmers and one or two small shops. Very little in the way of defenses, though."

"Okay, how about we start with the open road," Elijah suggested. "We can cross to the mountain path once we hit Borova."

"Works for me." Rue rolled up the map. "A word of caution. Don't trust anyone we meet along the way. If Mirov is on the warpath, then there are likely to be bounties on the heads of any Labyrinthine priests."

Elijah nodded. "Got it."

Rue left them and everyone finished their bread and water. The cups were replaced in packs and Elijah helped Sarin stand. Once the others were ready, Elijah slung his bow and quiver over his shoulder and started out of the enclosed valley. He picked a fairly clean path through the woods until they reached the open road. Wagon ruts, hoof prints, and human boot and footprints dotted the dirt.

Sarin tapped Elijah's shoulder and pointed

toward the right.

"It's gonna take me forever to get my bearings."

Sarin chuckled. "Just look up." Elijah did. "Timiria has one sun and two moons. Most folks tell time using them."

"That might have been helpful if I'd learned sailing," Elijah said. "Don't suppose Timirian dwarves learned how to make clocks, did they?"

"It's possible. Though I wouldn't venture into their strongholds to ask."

"Why not?"

Sarin shrugged as they walked. "Dwarves aren't particularly friendly to outsiders. Blame it on the last Timirian war. Humans and elves banded together to sweep dwarves back into the mountains. Some dwarves became slaves."

"Good God. Humans and elves couldn't think of anything else to do than pick on dwarves?"

"Well, you must understand," Sarin explained, "dwarves of Timiria are... well, warmongers. They seem to crave battle at any and all costs. When the Dwarven War -- the name for the campaign to force the dwarves back into the mountains -- began, it was because humans and elves had tired of the constant warfare dwarves brought to their cities."

"So... fight fire with fire."

"I suppose, yes."

Elijah snorted. "Sounds like most of the idiots in power on Earth."

"Idiocy would be a good word for it," Sarin said. "Not all humans and elves agreed with the war."

"Did you?"

"No. I have a few dwarven friends, though they've ceased living below ground. As a result, they were ostracized by their own people, and shunned by humans and elves. So most of them live very secluded, solitary existences."

"I think I'd prefer that over politics any day," Elijah said.

"It is why Elian built his cabin," Sarin said. "To stay clear of such nonsense."

"You haven't said much about how you feel," Elijah pointed out. "About this whole Elijah/Elian thing."

Sarin sighed and stared straight ahead, though his expression was one of thoughtfulness. "It is strange, I admit. You look exactly like him, you know. Every single detail. If someone were to look at you, they would never know the difference."

"I specifically created the character in the game to look like me," Elijah said. "As a character, he has a predetermined storyline, with a good bit of wiggle room. I never got too far into his personal story, though, because I focused on the overall main story. But that's not exactly what I was referring to."

"I know." Sarin glanced at him, giving Elijah a slight smile. "I love Elian, and if you are now him, then the same applies to you. I know you don't feel the same, given the circumstances, and I understand."

Elijah wasn't so sure he *didn't* feel the same. He felt like he'd known Sarin far longer than just a few days. "I'm not going to say I do, and I'm not going to say I don't. All I ask is for a little time to get things sorted out. For what it's worth, it's easy to see why Elian loves -- loved -- you, though."

They continued on with the rest of the group talking quietly behind them. A few of the kids whined a bit, but the adults kept them moving along. The road angled downward, though Elijah had no clue what direction they were headed. As the trees finally opened up, he almost stumbled to a stop.

"Oh, my God."

"Beautiful, isn't it?"

"No air pollution, no vehicles, no skyscrapers," Elijah said. "Just... nature." He started moving again before the others got antsy. "It's nothing like Earth."

"Is Earth that bad?" Sarin asked.

"It's crowded, and there are very few places with this much nature unless you go to a national park. I can see why other travelers haven't wanted to return to Earth."

They rounded a bend in the road and Elijah spotted a small cluster of people walking alongside a wagon, which was driven by a fifth person. All manner of goods filled the back of the wagon. As Elijah neared them, the ones walking stopped. The wagon followed suit and the driver twisted on the seat.

"Well, now," the driver said with a wide grin. "Don't see many travelers on the road these days."

Elijah started to ask how the man even knew he wasn't from Timiria, but then he realized the driver simply meant travelers in the broadest sense. "Good morning," Elijah said.

"Where might you all be headed?" the driver asked, looking at the men, women, and children behind Elijah.

Elijah glanced at Sarin, who just nodded. "Pelarum," Elijah answered. "We're on pilgrimage."

"Excellent!" The driver climbed down and dropped to the ground in a puff of dust. "Name's Edgar Mince," he said, extending a hand to Elijah. "Traveling salesman and purveyor of fortunes, at your service."

Elijah shook the man's hand, one eyebrow raised. "Purveyor of fortunes?"

"Yes, sir," Edgar said. He gestured to the people with him -- all four of them women. "My wives are all adept at discerning a fellow's -- or a lady's -- fortune."

"And your goods?" Elijah asked.

Edgar uncovered the stuff in the wagon and stepped back. Crystals glittered in the rising sunlight, and even without the aid of lighting them, Elijah could smell the various herbs and incense. "Little things," Edgar said. "Bits and pieces of healing crystals and soothing herbs I've collected in my travels. All for modest prices, of course."

Everyone in Elijah's little group began perusing the wares and chatting with Edgar's four wives. Elijah just stepped back, well away from the crowd. Even Rue and Sarin seemed intrigued.

"Not your type of entertainment?" Raig chuckled.

"I never put much thought into things like fortune-telling," Elijah admitted. "I take it you don't either."

"Not particularly. Rue likes to tease me on occasion about it."

"Aren't you a Laenassean priest, though?"

"Not all priests enjoy such things," Raig pointed out. "Some of us -- like Rue -- are the soothsayers, and, of course, being our Seer, it would make sense for Rue to be interested. But others -- like myself and Sarin -- are soldiers."

"Battlemages."

"I suppose you could call us that," Raig said. "We don't seek it out, but we are the ones on the front lines should the need arise. If this mess with Mirov reaches that point, rest assured that Sarin and I will be there, wielding our magic as surely as we swing our swords."

Sarin and Rue joined them off to the side. One of Edgar's wives wandered over as well. She bowed to them.

"Pardon me, sir," she said to Elijah, "but may I ask what your symbol means?"

"I..." Elijah didn't want to risk revealing the mages, so he went with the more convoluted answer. "I am not from Timiria."

Her face lit up. "You are a traveler!"

Several others turned toward him. Elijah groaned softly. "Yes, I am."

"I have only met one other like you," she said. "Oh, my apologies, sir. My name is Anelle." She lifted her skirt the slightest bit and curtsied.

Elijah bowed. "Elijah. Pleased to meet you. You have seen others like me?"

"Oh, yes, but he wasn't quite as kind as you are."

Elijah didn't like the sound of that. "What do you mean?"

"I've heard of travelers getting involved with the politics of Timiria, even working with the royal court," she said. "But rumor has it that there is a traveler who serves as King Mirov's top assassin. As foul as the traveler I met was, I wouldn't be surprised if he was the king's man."

"Does he have the same marking?" Elijah asked her.

She shook her head. "Different color, I think. And his glowed red, pulsing like a heartbeat."

Sarin's hand landed on Elijah's shoulder and squeezed. "I think it best we get moving."

"I agree." Elijah bowed to the woman, and then to Edgar and the man's other wives. "Ladies, gentlemen, children -- we should move on. I'm sure these good people have places to go and people to see as well."

Everyone wrapped up their business with Edgar, and then the salesman climbed back onto his wagon. He nodded in parting and led the wagon and his wives in the opposite direction they'd originally been going.

Elijah stared after them for a moment, unease settling in his gut about this king's assassin. "A traveler like me working as an assassin for the king," he muttered. "Not good."

"Agreed," Sarin said.

"A gamer is more likely to know little details about the game world and its people," Elijah said.

"Then it's even more imperative we get to Pelarum."

Chapter Three

Elijah had the feeling his good luck with this trek wouldn't last. About half an hour after their encounter with the merchant and the man's wives, the skies decided to put a damper on things. Thunder rumbled and lightning flashed overhead. Considering how he ended up in this world to begin with, Elijah had little desire to see where the next lightning strike landed him.

"We need to take shelter," he announced.

No one argued, not even the antsy kids. He spotted a cave a little ways up the side of the mountain to their right. Signaling the others to wait, he climbed up.

The cave was shallow with a visible back wall. Elijah sighed with relief. At least they wouldn't have to worry about anything sneaking up from the depths behind them. He waved at the group, and Sarin led them all up to the cave. The men and women got the kids settled and a small fire started with Rue's help. Elijah took watch at the entrance.

"I'd hoped to make better time," he said when Sarin sat down beside him. "But walking in lightning isn't smart, especially considering how I wound up here."

"I think the rest of them understand." Sarin handed him a cup of water. "I've been thinking about what Edgar's wife said, about the traveler she met once."

"Me, too," Elijah admitted. "And was it just me, or did something feel... off, with Edgar and his wives?"

Sarin sipped his own water and stared out at the

rain that had started coming down. "Having more than one spouse isn't unheard of here, but I am assuming you didn't quite mean that."

"The one wife we talked to seemed nice enough," Elijah said, "but Edgar was a bit... I don't know... weird."

"He looked vaguely familiar, though I can't place where I've seen him before."

"You were Captain of the Cosei guard," Elijah said. "Ever run into him before through that position?"

Sarin shrugged. "If I did, I don't recall."

Elijah sighed. The rain didn't seem to be letting up at all. He'd hoped they could've made it to Pelarum by the evening since Rue said it was only a day away. Now though, they were looking at a night huddling out of the storm.

Sarin shifted and sat behind Elijah, arms around Elijah's waist. "What I wouldn't give to be in Pelarum right now," he whispered. One hand slipped between Elijah's thighs, fingers just barely touching Elijah's balls through the thin pants.

Elijah groaned softly and managed to spread his legs a little more. "Sarin..."

"How quiet can *you* be?" Sarin unlaced Elijah's pants and worked his hand inside.

Warmth enveloped Elijah's cock, stealing his breath. "Oh, fuck..." he murmured.

He rocked into Sarin's fist, doing his absolute best to not hint at what they were doing. Sarin's breath heated the skin along the side of Elijah's neck, and kisses peppered the bend where his neck met his shoulder.

"I am envisioning myself inside you," Sarin whispered softly in Elijah's ear. "My cock thrusting, gliding in and out you."

Elijah's eyes rolled back and his balls drew tight. He had a damn good imagination. The promise of Sarin's words, the memory of the mage's knot locking inside him. Elijah's heartbeat sped up and he dug his fingers into Sarin's legs where they bracketed him.

"Sarin..."

Sarin's other hand slid into Elijah's pants and cupped his sac. Fingertips barely touched his hole, pressing just enough to drive him fucking crazy. The mage's hard cock pushed against Elijah, and Elijah swore he felt it flex.

Then the fingers pressed a bit harder, and Sarin's strokes quickened. Elijah bit his bottom lip and jerked. Spunk spilled over Sarin's fist and the mage groaned low. Warmth spread between them, no doubt ruining their clothes. Elijah couldn't bring himself to give a damn.

Sarin didn't move, just rested his head on Elijah's shoulders. "Thank Laenasse I have spare clothing," he muttered.

Elijah snorted. "The fun part is explaining *why* we need it."

"Perhaps we should go scout," Sarin suggested. "It would at least give us an excuse."

* * *

Thankfully, the rain stopped after only a couple of hours. Elijah got everyone moving again, though he kept an eye on the sky more now. They couldn't afford another lengthy break if they expected to reach Pelarum by nightfall. He remained alert as the road veered away from the general safety of the mountain range on one side and started down into the wide, open valley below.

Trees dotted the sprawling land, mingled with

patches of expansive fields, then climbed up along foothills and finally another mountain range on the far side. Elijah had no idea which direction he faced. Normally, at least on Earth, he'd had what amounted to an internal compass. Here, though, he was hopelessly confused.

"Okay, I give up," he said.

"Hmm?"

"Which direction is which?" he asked Sarin. He pointed toward the mountains they'd left, the ones that had been to their right.

"That is south," Sarin said.

"So that way is north," Elijah said, gesturing to the mountains and foothills far across the valley. Sarin nodded. Elijah hitched his thumb over one shoulder. "West?" he asked, motioning behind them.

"Yes. And we are headed east," Sarin answered.

"Good. Not that I'll ever remember any of it. You said there are dwarves, right?"

"Not the most hospitable of people, but, yes, there are dwarves."

"Maybe I can charm my way into getting a compass," Elijah mused.

"You really should learn the sun and moons. Not only do they help us tell time, they indicate directions."

That made sense. "Does the Timirian sun rise in the east and set in the west?"

"Yes, it does."

Elijah let out a sigh of relief. "Then maybe there's hope for me after all. Some guide I am."

Sarin laughed and slipped an arm around Elijah's waist. "You're doing what needs to be done, love. I doubt anyone cares about your lack of direction so long as we have a map and someone who knows which way to go."

"Gee, thanks."

They continued on in silence, with only the occasional snippet of conversation coming from behind them, for the next couple of hours. The weather held up, affording an even more magnificent view of the valley into which they descended. Although Elijah spotted a few farmsteads and ruins of old fortresses, he didn't see anything that remotely resembled a still-functioning town.

Another hour of walking led to the kids complaining of being tired. Elijah stopped and turned, ready to announce a break, when he heard what sounded like someone running -- toward them.

"To the side!"

He ushered everyone behind a cluster of boulders, then crouched behind a bush, bow at the ready. The footsteps grew closer and he realized the person was running. He nocked an arrow, just in case. Then the figure crested the small hill of the road.

"Anelle?"

One of Edgar's wives, the one Elijah had met, stopped. Her eyes widened, and Elijah lowered his bow. She looked like she'd run the entire way.

"What are you doing here?"

"Please, sir -- Elijah," she panted. "My husband does not know I am gone. I left when he was busy with a farmer."

Elijah waved her out of the middle of the road and toward the boulders where the others hid. "Why are you here?"

"To warn you," Anelle said. "My husband is not who he claims to be."

The uneasiness returned, and this time Elijah didn't ignore it outright. "What do you mean? Who is he?"

"He is in the service of King Mirov. His job is to wander the open roads and relay what he finds -- and who he finds -- back to the king."

Elijah cursed under his breath. "Does he know what I am?"

"I don't know," Anelle said. "All I know is that he has orders to report anyone suspicious to the king. When you left us, he mentioned doing just that regarding you and your companions."

"Oh, God," Elijah groaned. "What about you? Are you really one of his wives? And what will happen when he realizes you're gone?"

"I am one of them, yes, though not by choice." Anelle sighed at Elijah's confused look. "I was married off to him as a result of a land deal. I don't know how they do such things in your world, but here, there are places in Timiria, other areas like where Edgar is from, where women are property."

"That's ridiculous!"

"There are many who agree with you," Anelle said. "But even the king has multiple wives gained in similar ways. It is one reason we are at war."

Elijah glanced briefly at Sarin, then back to Anelle. "One reason?"

"Rumors abound that the Laenassean priests have allied themselves with one of Mirov's rivals. If that rival manages to sway the people, then she will have a stronger contest to the throne."

Elijah blinked. "She?"

Anelle nodded. "Princess Elsbeth," she said. "Mirov's exiled sister."

Elijah had the feeling he just landed in even more hot water than he'd originally thought. "Okay, let me get this straight. You know I'm a traveler." She nodded. "I wound up here because I was playing a game -- a game set in this world. The big, all-encompassing storyline mentioned nothing about a war between the king and his sister. It was supposed to be about some fabled jewel."

He froze, a thought occurring to him. "Oh, my God. She is the jewel!"

"Pardon?" Anelle asked.

"Elsbeth -- she's the jewel," Elijah said. "The game box said 'a precious jewel, lost and forgotten, that will forever change life in Timiria should it return.' That's referring to Elsbeth. She was lost to the people, forgotten by her brother, and if she returns, her rule would change Timiria."

Anelle regarded him with a curious expression. "You may be right," she said. "I know nothing about a jewel, but Elsbeth is well-loved by many people. But to speak her name is to commit treason in Mirov's eyes."

"I imagine so," Elijah said. "What do you have to do with all of this?"

"I am merely with Edgar as a servant," Anelle said. "The newest -- and thus, the lowest -- of his wives."

"And if you are found to be gone?"

Anelle swallowed. "I will be executed."

Elijah nodded. "I figured that. You're coming with us."

"Are you certain?"

"I'm not about to leave you out here alone, Anelle." Elijah looked to Sarin, Rue, and Raig. All three men nodded, giving their blessings. "Welcome to our little caravan."

* * *

By nightfall, they were within sight of Pelarum. Elijah stopped for a moment, giving the others a chance to rest, and just gazed down at the decent-sized town. He couldn't wait to collapse onto a real bed, preferably under Sarin.

"When I first discovered I had the gift of Sight, I feared it."

Elijah glanced over at Ruelaeri. "Why?"

"I didn't want to know things others did not," Rue said. "I wanted to be normal, to be like the other boys in my village."

"What is it like, being the Seer?"

"It can be a blessing at times -- now," Rue answered. "But there are moments when I wish I didn't have the gift. I knew Sarin's mother -- my dear friend Kala -- was going to die before it happened. There was nothing I could do to save her. I prayed to Laenasse, begged the Goddess to spare my sweet friend, but it was not to be."

"Did she get to see Sarin before she died? He said it happened minutes after his birth."

"She held him but then gave him to me. She knew," Rue said, looking over at Elijah. "She knew she was dying."

Elijah sighed and gazed down at Pelarum. The sun had almost set completely. "I'm sorry."

"Kala was a special woman, and she gave me the greatest gift of all: my son."

Elijah smiled at that. "I can't complain either."

"Sarin has the gift of Sight as well," Rue said, "but he refuses to use it."

"What?" Elijah stared at Rue. "Why?"

"For much the same reason I didn't want to at first, I imagine."

"It makes sense," Elijah said. "You have it, so it's not surprising he inherited it."

"Anelle did not tell you everything."

"Huh?"

Rue smirked, but didn't look at Elijah. "Mirov banished his sister because she, like us, possesses magic."

"Well, that explains why he despises mages."

"Do not let Anelle out of your sight," Rue warned.

"Do you think she's dangerous?"

Rue finally looked at Elijah. "No. She is in *danger*."

Chapter Four

Even at night, Pelarum bustled with activity. Shopkeepers were starting to close up their shops, but customers lingered everywhere. Kids and animals -- dogs, goats, chickens, pigs, and even one cow -- all wound up underfoot, or blocking entire spaces in the cow's case. Only a few people paused long enough to watch the newcomers make their way through the main gate, but then the townsfolk returned to whatever they'd been doing.

Elijah ignored them as best he could, trying not to bring attention to himself. Rue said Pelarum's lord was no fan of Mirov, but considering Elian's reputation, Elijah had no desire to test that theory. He followed Sarin's directions toward the keep at the top of a large, central hill.

When they got to the front gate, guards bowed and opened it for them without blinking an eye. Elijah didn't know what to make of it. He walked through and halted mid-step.

Rows and rows of men and women, dressed for battle, stood at attention while officers inspected them. These weren't guards. Each soldier held a spear, a sword and shield, or a bow. From the towering main keep, a tall, muscular figure emerged. A dark blue cape fluttered in the breeze behind him, just barely touching the dirt ground. Elijah didn't need an introduction to know this was the Lord of Pelarum. The man exuded power and control.

"Rue, my friend," the lord announced as he neared. He grinned, breaking the icy, serious demeanor. "I'm so glad you're alive."

Rue shook the man's hand. "Just barely. Ordul is

gone. Our newest Sentinel --" He gestured to Elijah, "--got us out without trouble."

The lord smiled and approached Elijah, extending a hand. "Lord Aven," he said. "I am pleased to meet you, Sentinel."

Elijah shook Aven's hand. "As am I. Elijah, please."

"Elijah it is." Aven released him and waved toward the keep. "Come. I'm sure you're all quite famished and tired." Aven led them into the great hall, which was already full of people. Servants hurried to Aven's side and he issued instructions before turning back to Elijah and the others. "Make yourselves at home. Mirov cannot reach you here." He started to return to his chair on the dais when he froze. His gaze locked onto Anelle. "My lady…"

Elijah blinked and stepped aside. He watched as Aven kissed the top of Anelle's hand.

"I had thought you dead, your Highness."

Had it not been for the wall behind him, Elijah would have hit the floor. "Highness?"

Anelle glanced at him, her expression apologetic. "I am sorry for the deception," she said.

"Who *are* you?"

"My birth name was Elsbeth."

"You're the queen?" Elijah almost shouted. He winced, but no one seemed to notice what he'd said. "Why in God's name were you out in the wild with a creep like Edgar?"

"No one knows what Elsbeth looks like anymore," she said. "I had to see what my brother knew, what he is planning."

"You've risked your…" Elijah shook his head. "I can't believe I just escorted the future queen of Timiria across the countryside. What do I even call you?"

"For now, call me Anelle. When the time comes for me to take back the throne, then all will know who I am."

"So…" Elijah glanced around at the people in the great hall. "What about these people?"

She smiled and lifted a hand. The air shimmered around Elijah, Anelle, Aven, and Sarin. "I am sure your lover's father has told you why I was banished. Mirov fears my magic, and rightly so. I erected a barrier when we entered the great hall, shielding the four of us from the ears of the others. Imagine what I could do with an army of my brother's men."

"It's official," Elijah said. "You rock."

Anelle raised one eyebrow. "I am assuming that is a good thing in your world."

Elijah laughed. "Yeah, it is. A very good thing."

* * *

Elijah fell backward onto the bed. "I'm never eating again."

Sarin chuckled and crawled onto the bed, between Elijah's thighs. "You cannot be that full."

"I ate more in one sitting than I have in the past several days, Sarin."

Sarin bent down and nuzzled Elijah's neck. "I suppose I could just leave you to nap --"

"Like hell," Elijah interrupted. He grabbed a hand of Sarin's hair and tugged the mage into a kiss. One of them groaned -- hell, maybe both of them. Elijah somehow got his other hand between their bodies and rubbed his fingers up and down the hardening length of Sarin's cock, trapped beneath the mage's pants. "Get naked."

Sarin pulled away and stood. Elijah lay back and watched as the mage stripped down to nothing within seconds. The patterns of blue fur made Elijah's pulse quicken, and the sight of Sarin's thick cock made Elijah's entire body tighten.

"Your turn."

Elijah got rid of his own clothing, tossing it in random directions. Then he locked both legs around Sarin's waist and jerked. Sarin fell onto him with a grunt, pressing their cocks together. Elijah moaned and lifted his hips, rocking against Sarin.

"I could easily come like this," Elijah murmured. "Just rubbing on you."

"Likewise." Sarin reached over to the small pack he'd put on the bed and retrieved a vial. He held up the small container. "But I think being inside is much more enticing."

Grinning, Elijah unlocked his legs and spread them. Sarin slicked two fingers, then leaned down, easing them both into Elijah's ass. Elijah gasped, eyes rolling back.

"Oh, fuck…" he whispered. "More."

"As you wish." Sarin added a third and Elijah shivered. Sarin twisted and turned his hand, working Elijah open. "Please tell me you're ready."

"God, yes." Elijah grabbed the backs of his thighs and held his legs up and apart. "Now."

Sarin withdrew his fingers, lined up his cock, and pushed. They both moaned as he sank in to the hilt. Elijah panted and Sarin waited. At Elijah's nod, Sarin began moving. The knot formed a second or two later. Every stroke, every thrust, pulled and tugged, Sarin's cock plunging in deep before pulling the knot just to the entrance.

"Fuck," Elijah gasped. "Harder. Please!"

Sarin kissed Elijah and slammed into him. Elijah cried out, the sound muffled. He hooked his legs around Sarin, freeing his hands. Sarin grabbed both and pinned them to the bed. Elijah held on, heart thundering as the mage pistoned in and out of his ass. Each glide drove Elijah fucking insane. The knot rubbed his prostate over and over.

Elijah tore away from the kiss and shouted. Spunk shot onto his stomach. Sarin let out a feral growl and rocked into him. Thick heat pulsed inside Elijah, filling him. His head swam, and he felt torn between dizziness and ecstasy.

Sarin finally slowed, then eased out. When Elijah managed to catch his breath, he looked over at his lover, only to find Sarin watching him.

Something caught in Elijah's throat -- something important, stronger than anything else he'd ever felt.

Sarin smiled and caressed Elijah's cheek with one hand. "Sometimes," Sarin said. "Words aren't needed."

Chapter Five

The next morning, Elijah found himself sitting at a table full of people he didn't know, save for Rue, Raig, and Sarin. The others he'd led from Ordul were nowhere to be seen, and even Anelle and Aven had yet to show themselves. Elijah had a sneaking suspicion why, at least for those two. He leaned to the side, voice lowering to a whisper when he spoke to Sarin.

"Is it just me, or is there something going on between Anelle -- Elsbeth -- and Aven?"

"I'm surprised it took you that long to figure it out," Sarin replied with a chuckle. "Before her disappearance, rumors ran rampant about Princess Elsbeth and her love of a lesser lord. Needless to say, her parents weren't particularly pleased."

"What did happen to her parents? How did Mirov get the throne?"

"Mirov is younger than Elsbeth by only a few minutes," Sarin said. He glanced at Elijah. "They're twins. As for their parents, many people speculate that Mirov eventually murdered their father, King Elan. No one knows how Queen Fiondra died, though it's said she was murdered as well."

"So Mirov murders both parents, then usurps a throne that rightly belongs to his sister. I take it men don't automatically inherit thrones in Timiria."

"In many holds, it's up to the lords as to who -- and how -- their successors are named, but the royal court is... an entity unto itself. Women are just as likely to take the throne as men, and evil minds can inhabit either gender. Mirov isn't the first monarch to rule in such a way."

"It's a miracle the system works at all," Elijah

grumbled. "Makes me damn glad I'm not royalty."

"Believe me," Sarin said. "I've said the same thing many times. I have no desire to play the political games of the royal court. Lords are bad enough in their own right, but the royal house is beyond compare."

A door near the dais opened and everyone stood, Elijah included. Aven, with Anelle's hand on his arm, descended the steps to join them all at the breakfast table. He helped her to her seat, then took his own. Everyone sat back down.

"I want to thank you all for meeting with me this morning," Aven said. "Each one of you, I trust implicitly." He looked to each of them in turn, finally settling on Elijah. "Elijah, I know you are new to us -- to Timiria."

Elijah waited for a moment, expecting at least a whisper or two. No one said a word. He nodded. "Yes."

"Everyone here, at one time or another, served Princess Elsbeth before her exile." He smiled and lifted Anelle's hand, kissing the back of it. "Rest assured, her identity is safe with them all."

"That's good to know," Elijah said.

Anelle laughed. "Indeed."

"So now that we're here, what are we going to do?" Elijah asked.

"Gather our allies," Raig said.

Rue added, "And our strength. We need to rebuild the priesthood."

"There is an older temple in the village," Aven told them. "No one has used it for some time. I can't say it's perfect, but it may suit your needs. Of course, you will have whatever resources I can provide."

"And Mirov?" Elijah asked. "We met a merchant -- Edgar -- on the road. We found out, thanks to Anelle

-- Elsbeth -- that he is, in essence, a scout for the king. If he reports back to Mirov about us, then Mirov may send troops looking for any of us."

Aven sat back and seemed to ponder the question. "There are neighboring holds ruled by lords who, like myself, bear no love for Mirov. We need to get word to them. I will hold a meeting and explain the situation. I do not doubt they will listen to reason."

Elijah didn't need to ask who would be the one to go on those quests. "Just tell me how to get to each one."

"I would ask how you knew I was going to suggest you be the one to go, but something tells me the answer is a bit... complicated," Aven said.

Elijah chuckled and shook his head. "You have no idea."

"I'll go with you," Sarin told him. "I know where the holds are, and I can conceal us if we encounter any of the king's men."

"Works for me." Elijah looked back to Aven. "Any thoughts on what I should say?"

"Just tell them Lord Aven is calling a meeting here in Pelarum. They will come."

Elijah hoped it was that simple, but he'd been through similar quests in games. He knew better. "All right. When do we leave?"

* * *

Elijah packed what he'd need for the trip. He had no clue how long they'd be gone, but he assumed it would be several days.

"Aven is providing us with two of his finest horses," Sarin said. He shut the door and set his own pack on the bed.

"That'll help." Elijah tied the pack closed. "I

would ask how long you think we'll be traveling from hold to hold, but in my gaming experience, these sorts of quests are never simple."

"What do you mean?"

Elijah sat on the bed. "Well, in a game, if the storyline involves going from place to place to get help, whether it's resources or to build an army, you -- the gamer, that is -- have to prove your worth, so to speak. The lords or kings of those places have you go out to do this quest or that quest, or even several in a series, before they'll even consider what you have to say."

Sarin snorted. "Sounds like Timirian politics in general."

"I honestly have no clue what to expect," Elijah said, "but I'm basically planning on pretty much that happening. We get to the first hold, and the lord will have us do this or that -- or several thats -- before he'll agree to Aven's meeting."

"One thing you have to understand about Timiria," Sarin replied. "Nothing is free here. There is always something to trade or barter, something someone wants in exchange for what you want."

"Makes sense, though I can see how things can get unbalanced real fast."

"And they do, believe me," Sarin said. "The fight over the royal throne is the perfect example of that."

"What sort of queen do you think she would make?"

Sarin shrugged. "I honestly don't know. She's certainly nicer than her twin, but I don't know her."

Elijah chewed on his lower lip, unsure if he should ask his next question.

"You look pensive, love. What is it?"

"Rue said you have the same gift. Sight."

Sarin groaned and fell backward onto the bed.

"My father talks too much."

Elijah lay back, propped on his arm beside Sarin. "But it's true, right?"

"Yes," Sarin sighed.

"Why do you not want to use it?"

"Did he tell you about my mother?"

"He said he knew she was going to die before it happened," Elijah answered.

"Right... and he couldn't stop it." Sarin closed his eyes. "I can't let myself see the future. I fear I'll see something like he did, and there won't be anything I can do to change it. We control our destinies, but sometimes Fate has other ideas."

"What if seeing the future can help us prepare for this war?" Elijah asked. "I would think any warning is better than no warning."

Sarin stared at him for several seconds before speaking. "You're really asking me to do this, aren't you?"

"We need all the help we can get, Sarin," Elijah argued.

Sarin dragged both hands down his face and grumbled. "Fine." He motioned for Elijah to get up. When Elijah did, Sarin knelt on the floor, hands on his thighs, palms up. He closed his eyes and, after a few moments, his breathing slowed to almost nothing.

Elijah didn't know what to expect, so he sat back and watched. Sarin didn't move, except for the very shallow, very slow rise and fall of his chest as he breathed. Then the air in the room began to change. Elijah felt it crawl over his skin, like tiny little ghost fingers. He'd felt Sarin's magic during sex, but this was different.

A pale blue light formed around Sarin's body, pulsing in time to every inhale and exhale he took.

Elijah had never seen an aura, but he figured that's what this was, or at least something similar.

Sarin seemed to relax a bit more. The temperature changed, going from comfortably warm to cool within a few seconds. Elijah swore Sarin had simply gone somewhere else, in spirit anyway.

A few moments later, Sarin gasped. The sound startled Elijah and he crouched in front of Sarin. The mage didn't look like he even saw Elijah there.

"Sarin?"

Sarin stared straight through him. "Mirov knows who you are. Edgar told him. There is a price on your head, and on Anelle's. Mirov believes you both will bring about his downfall." The mage's eyes finally focused on Elijah, but the expression in them chilled Elijah to the bone. "Mirov has sent his top assassin to find you -- here, in Pelarum. We're not safe here. *You* aren't safe here."

* * *

"Are you certain of this?"

"Yes," Elijah said. "Sarin confirmed it. Mirov's assassin -- a traveler like me -- is somewhere in Pelarum. The assassin knows who I am. He's after me… and Anelle."

Aven gripped the arms of his chair on the dais. "Does this assassin know who Anelle is?"

"No," Sarin said as he walked into the great hall. He looked far more rested now. Using the Sight had drained him of a good bit of energy. "Anelle's identity remains that of a wayward wife, though she's been branded a traitor. Mirov doesn't know she's Elsbeth under glamor."

"We can't fight what we can't see," Aven said. "How do we find this assassin?"

"We give him what he wants," Anelle said. All eyes turned to her.

"Have you lost your mind?" Aven asked. "I lost you once. I will not lose you again -- permanently!"

"Do you expect me to sit idly by and wait like a simpering weakling?" Anelle shot back. She stood and went down the steps of the dais. Then she pivoted on her heel. "I am not some wallflower waiting to be plucked and crushed. I was young when my brother exiled me, but that was years ago. Do you really think I've spent the past years doing nothing but follow Edgar around?"

Aven held up both hands in surrender. "All right, all right, I concede. I don't like it, but I know when to shut up."

"Good." Anelle turned to Elijah. "If Mirov's assassin is looking for us, then finding him will be easy. Use me as bait. I can play the simple woman card. You will wait until he has me, then take him down. Don't kill him. We need him to talk."

"In my world, you'd be a kick-ass special agent."

Anelle laughed. "And again, I'm taking that as a compliment."

"So..." Elijah surveyed the others. "When and how do we do this?"

Chapter Six

"I can't believe I agreed to this."

"Shh!"

Elijah scowled, but Anelle ignored him. He'd dressed as himself but kept his tattoo halfway visible in hopes it would alert the assassin. Anelle had changed clothes as well, more in line with the lower status a merchant's wife would be. "You're a queen," he muttered. "You're going to get yourself killed."

"I'm going to shove my dingy, peasant woman boot up your rear if you don't pipe down."

Elijah barely stifled a chuckle. Anelle was nothing like he'd expected a queen to be. "Fine. But I still say this is stupid."

"You're entitled to your opinion," Anelle murmured. She peered around the corner. Then she motioned for Elijah. He joined her. "See him?"

Across the narrow street, a hooded figure stood, watching the people pass by in all directions. Although his clothing style fit well with those around him, something about him made him stand out from all others.

"Ready?"

Elijah wanted to say no. "Yes."

Anelle didn't wait after that. She left her hiding place and strolled into the street, as if perusing the various wares nestled in shop stalls. The hooded man watched her closely. When she stepped behind a curtain, on the pretense of looking at more goods, he made his move. Elijah barely stopped himself from darting out the second the assassin's hand clamped tight over Anelle's mouth, stopping any potential scream. He whispered something in her ear and she nodded, eyes wide in mock fright.

Elijah waited while the assassin dragged her into one of the many storehouses throughout the town. Then he left his place and followed as quickly and quietly as possible. He drew one dagger and peered around the door frame.

"Do you think your snooping and whispering have gone unnoticed?" The assassin circled Anelle, who knelt on the floor, hands bound behind her back. "Your pathetic excuse of a husband ratted you out, but Mirov's had his eye on you. He thinks you're a threat." The assassin leaned down and sneered. "I think you're much more than meets the eye..." Anelle met the man's gaze. "... your Highness."

Elijah's blood ran ice cold. Fuck! He slipped into the storehouse, grip tightening on the dagger. Anelle didn't move a muscle, just stared up at the assassin.

"That's right. Mirov might not know the truth, but, you see, I know things he doesn't." The assassin parted his shirt to reveal a red tattoo identifying him as a traveler. "In my world, there are these wonderful things called cheat codes and walkthroughs. I know who you are. I know what you're planning. And I know --"

"That you aren't the only traveler," Elijah growled, knife pressed precariously to the assassin's throat.

"Do you really think I'm the only one who took this side of the story? Do you honestly believe I'll tell you a damn thing?"

"It doesn't matter," Elijah said. "You might have read through the walkthroughs and entered the cheat codes, but I have the mages. If you don't talk voluntarily, I'm quite sure they'll make you do so without your consent."

Elijah felt the assassin swallow against the blade.

"Now I'm going to tell you this one time," Elijah said. "Untie her. If you try anything stupid, I won't hesitate to let her roast you to a fucking crisp."

He removed the knife and the assassin did exactly as instructed. Then Elijah grabbed the assassin's hands and bound them behind the man's back with a length of rope Anelle handed him. Just as he started to turn the man around toward the door, Anelle hauled her arm back and nailed the assassin in the jaw. The assassin howled in pain, crumpling to the floor.

"That's for picking the wrong twin, you son of a bitch."

* * *

"Can I torch him yet?"

Aven did the classic face-palm move, and Elijah tried not to laugh. Anelle had been itching to "torch" the assassin since they got the man to the keep. With every passing moment, Elijah liked her more and more. Aven, apparently, wasn't as enthusiastic about turning the assassin into a human barbeque just yet.

"I take it he's not talking," Aven said.

"Nope." Elijah leaned against the one of the huge columns in the great hall. "Though, from what we gathered in the storehouse, Mirov doesn't know Anelle is Elsbeth, but our assassin does. My question is, who else knows? I'm not the only traveler. If one gamer chose Mirov's side, then it's safe to say others did as well."

"I know," Aven sighed. "What are our options, besides immolation?"

Anelle huffed and crossed her arms.

"There's one option," Rue said, smirking at

Anelle. "One that doesn't involve fire at all, I might add."

Aven met Rue's gaze. "I'm listening."

"While Sarin and I have the gift of Sight, Raig possesses the ability to mind-read. We don't need this assassin to talk."

"Where's the fun in that?" Anelle grumbled.

"I'll show you plenty of fun later," Aven shot back. Anelle grinned.

Rue rolled his eyes at them both. "I will send Raig down to the dungeon."

Elijah followed Rue out of the great hall. "You think this will work?"

"I know it will. Raig only uses the ability when absolutely necessary, but it's highly effective."

Raig met them in the hall. "Let's get this over with before Anelle decides to go about it her way."

Sarin joined them and they all went down into the dungeon. Elijah ignored the cells lining both sides of the corridor. He had no desire whatsoever to see who or what might be lurking inside. When they reached the only closed door, Rue produced a key. He unlocked the door and pushed it open. Raig went in first and the others followed.

The assassin sat on the stone floor, chains on his wrists and ankles, and scowled up at them. "Time for the torture?"

Raig crouched and, without giving the assassin a chance to move, grabbed the man's head.

"Hey! What the fuck?" The assassin jerked, eyes going wide. The man's pupils glazed over and he began shaking.

"Mirov doesn't know Anelle is Elsbeth," Raig relayed, "but he's growing suspicious. There are six other travelers working for the king: two more secondary assassins, two advisors, and one bounty hunter. This one is Jacob. Michael and Kyle are the two other assassins. He doesn't know the names of the advisors or bounty hunter. He hasn't told Mirov about Anelle's identity, but the others -- and Mirov -- know about Elijah. They know the Coseian Shadow is alive and well."

Raig released the assassin and the man slumped against the wall, eyes closed and drool pooling in the corner of his mouth. Raig stood.

"He'll be fine after a day or so. What are we going to do with him?"

Rue studied the assassin. "We will leave that up to Aven and Anelle. For now, I believe it is time to revise our initial meeting plan."

They all left the dungeon and headed back up to the great hall. Once there, Raig relayed the information he'd gathered from the assassin's mind.

"I still need the others," Aven said. "We need the meeting."

"Sarin and I can get to the holds by horseback fairly quickly," Elijah said.

"Do it," Aven said. "Tell the lords it's imperative they come. Mirov isn't going to wait once he discovers his prize assassin is missing."

Elijah nodded and followed Sarin back to their room. "Well, time to go, I guess."

Sarin dragged him close for a kiss. "At least you aren't going alone."

Elijah grinned. "So true."

LinkDead (DungeonCrawl 3)

Mychael Black

Elijah Burrows and his lover, Sarin, are off to do the unthinkable: offer their services to their enemy.

King Mirov's assassin failed, and Elijah and Sarin hope to spy on the monarch by posing as for-hire mercenaries. With a new, magic-induced appearance and Sarin acting as a wolf companion, Elijah journeys to Mirov's palace in the neighboring province and convinces Mirov he's available and ready to do anything to aid the throne.

What could possibly go wrong?

Chapter One

There were times when Elijah wondered if he'd been better off in his own world, as opposed to Timiria. Now was one of those times. They'd all managed to gain a bit of insight into King Mirov's plans, including his use of other travelers -- gamers trapped in the world of Timiria. Now they had to figure out just what the hell to do. Mirov had them outnumbered, despite the return of Elsbeth, Mirov's sister and rightful ruler of Timiria. The whole notion of war made Elijah queasy.

Strong hands rested on Elijah's shoulders, massaging the tension right out of them. He sighed and leaned back against his lover, the lupine mage Sarin. Since getting thrown into this world, Elijah had nearly been decapitated, almost turned into a pincushion by arrows, and came too damn close to the wrong end of an orc's sword. Through it all, though, he'd come back to this one man, ready for whatever sort of healing Sarin offered. Elijah knew Sarin loved the game character Elian -- the one Elijah had created to play the game -- and as time went by, Elijah realized he was slowly falling for the mage, too. Taking over Elian's life had been a bit weird, but finding out the thief character had a lover was a pleasant bonus.

"You haven't said much this past hour, Elijah." Ruelaeri, Sarin's father and the Labyrinthine Order's Seer, turned his attention to Elijah. All others followed suit, putting Elijah on the spot. "Any insight, given your experience with this world through a game?"

Elijah opened his mouth to answer, only to realize he really had no clue what to say. He sighed. "I honestly don't know. I never made it very far into the main plotline of the game's story. DungeonCrawl's plot centered on a fabled jewel -- which I now suspect referred to Elsbeth and not an actual gem -- but beyond that, I don't know anything about war or battle. The little fighting I've done since I got here has been, for the most part, one on one, with the exception of a few bandits and spiders the size of a damn horse."

Sarin chuckled, and Elijah resisted the urge to elbow the man in the ribs. Getting used to the wildlife of Timiria presented almost as much of a challenge as learning how to scout.

"What about the other travelers?" Raig, Rue's lover, asked. "Do you know them?"

"Not a single one. On Earth, people all over the world play games like DungeonCrawl. For all I know, the travelers here lived on opposite sides of the planet. I can tell you that our... guest downstairs is definitely American, though. He has a strong New York accent, even if he's been here longer than I have."

"From your expression, I'm going to wager a guess that New York is not one of your favorite places," Rue remarked.

Elijah grimaced. "Hate it. Too noisy, too crowded, too dirty."

"So what do we do?" Elsbeth asked. "My brother is going to wonder what happened when his assassin doesn't return. Mirov isn't known for his patience, either. Where one assassin failed, another two may try to take his place."

Elijah had been thinking about it for a while now, since they dragged the traveler-turned-assassin down into the dungeon for questioning. "Well... there's one possible idea, though I'm probably completely insane for even considering it."

"Yes?" Aven, Elsbeth's lover, asked.

"I'm not cut out for battle, but I can be sneaky as hell. What are the chances of me 'enlisting' in Mirov's service, as a spy?"

Sarin's posture turned rigid behind him. "Are you out of your mind?"

"On the contrary," Rue said with a grin, "I think it's a brilliant idea."

"If Mirov suspects even the slightest that Elijah is one of ours, we all pay a hefty price and I lose the love of my life!"

Elijah gripped Sarin's hand and gave it a gentle squeeze. "Babe, I won't go alone." He smiled at Sarin's narrowed gaze. "How long can you stay in wolf form?"

"For as long as I need to," Sarin muttered.

"We can use that to our advantage. I'll change my appearance -- somehow -- go to Mirov, and offer my services as an assassin or scout -- with the help of my trusty wolf companion."

"You're completely insane."

"Unsurprisingly, you aren't the first one to tell me that." Elijah laughed. "Hell, you aren't the first boyfriend to say it."

Sarin sighed and rested his head on Elijah's shoulder. "I can't believe I'm agreeing to this," he grumbled. "When do we leave?"

"The sooner, the better." Rue got up, bowed to Elsbeth, and then nodded to Elijah and Sarin. "Come with me. Between myself and Sarin, we can relay information telepathically from a distance, and I will figure out some way to change your appearance."

Elijah and Sarin stood from the table and bowed to the others. Then they followed Rue out of the great hall. The keep of Pelarum wasn't huge, but it still reminded Elijah of castles he'd seen in pictures and movies. Rue led them down one corridor and into the room he shared with Raig.

"First things first," Rue said as he turned. He lifted both hands and closed his eyes. He murmured -- chanted, more like -- under his breath.

Elijah felt the air around his body vibrate, and his skin tingled. He glanced down and blinked, eyes going wide as his skin darkened to a light bronze -- far darker than his usual paleness. He'd never been able to get even the slightest tan before now.

"Dude, you'd make a killing with the housewives in California."

Sarin snorted and poked him to hush. Rue continued chanting.

Elijah looked in the mirror behind Rue and watched as his short, spiky brown hair turned pitch black and lengthened to his shoulders. "Wow," he mouthed.

Rue stopped and took a deep breath before sitting on the bed. He gestured at Elijah. "It should last for some time," he said, a bit breathless. "If it begins to fade, Sarin can reinforce it."

"Are you all right?" Elijah asked.

Rue nodded. "I will be. It takes a good bit of energy to cast a glamour on someone else -- especially something strong enough to hold for an extended period of time."

"How long do we have before it starts to weaken?"

"A month," Rue said. "I honestly don't know how long you two will be gone." He met Sarin's gaze. "Son... please be cautious."

Sarin crouched in front of Rue and took his father's hands in both of his. "I will. Stay safe, please."

Rue smiled. "Pack your things, and I will see you

out the main gate."

* * *

"Mirov's palace is just outside the city of Cosei --
where Elian was born," Rue explained. "How much do
you remember from your time playing the game?"

Elijah had to think about it for a moment. "Cosei
is in the neighboring province, Erona, right? South of
Tasmorum?"

"Correct." Rue handed Sarin a pack containing
enough food to last through the trip to Cosei. "Stick to
the well-traveled roads -- less chance of running into
trouble out in the open. The Ethur Mountains bisect the
Tasmorum province, and you should be able to take
shelter in Segorus. It's a small town that serves as the
waypoint between North and South Tasmorum."

"My sense of direction is still a bit off here,"
Elijah said. "How far from Segorus is Cosei?"

"About two days," Sarin answered. "I'll stay in
wolf form and lead the way. Better protection, too."

Elijah snorted. "Protection? More like no one will
step foot near me with a horse-sized wolf playing
guard."

Sarin grinned. "Exactly."

Elijah climbed up onto the saddle of Shail, the
horse he'd borrowed from Aven. Sarin hugged Rue
one last time, then shifted into wolf form. The wolf's
shoulders almost reached the horse's back in height.
Nope, not a chance in hell of any bandit attacks, for
sure. Rue waved and Elijah turned the horse toward
what he hoped was the south. Sarin nudged the horse's
flank, then took off at a loping gait in the same
direction. Elijah's horse followed.

* * *

They traveled for what felt like several hours

before Sarin veered off into the woods. Confused, Elijah guided the horse in after him. They moved along a narrow path and then into a small outcropping of enormous boulders. A cave entrance came into view around one of the boulders. Sarin sat at the entrance and seemed to nod toward the opening. Elijah dismounted and led the horse into the cave.

It wasn't very deep, and it felt damp and cold. However, it was definitely sheltered. Sarin shifted, and Elijah couldn't help but watch the process. It looked like it hurt, but Sarin didn't make any sort of expression hinting at pain. The mage dug into one of their packs and pulled out a tiny pouch.

"I need to find a few small sticks for a fire," Sarin said. He tossed the pouch to Elijah. "Make a circle with any loose stones you can find -- just not too big. The less light, the better. I'll be right back." He shifted once more and ducked out of the cave before Elijah could blink.

Elijah scoured the back of the cave and gathered several small and medium-sized rocks. He arranged them in a circle, then sat and waited. Curiosity got the better of him and he carefully opened the pouch.

"Dust?"

"Flash powder." Sarin returned, in human form again, and piled the sticks in the center of the circle. "Take a pinch, then toss it onto the wood."

Elijah eyed him, skeptical. "You're joking."

"Not at all."

Not expecting much, Elijah got a small bit of the dust and sprinkled it onto the sticks. Flames roared and he jerked his hand back, the hairs on his skin nearly singed. "Holy fuck!"

Sarin laughed. "I could do it with magic, but the powder requires no energy from me."

Elijah handed the pouch back to Sarin -- very carefully. "Dare I ask what happens if you drop that?"

Sarin let the pouch hit the rock floor of the cave, sending Elijah's heart straight into his damn throat. Nothing happened.

"What the hell?"

"It only works on wood," Sarin explained. "And the powder must come into direct contact. In the leather pouch, on rock, it's completely harmless."

"That... could be useful."

"I daresay it will be eventually. Raig created it years ago. Did you notice any burn marks throughout his keep when we were there?"

Now that Elijah thought about it, he had. "Didn't really think much about them. Figured they were part of a battle."

"Nope." Sarin chuckled. "Tests."

"I would ask what Rue thought of such tests, but something tells me your father probably encouraged them."

"He picked the targets."

Elijah just shook his head. Sarin was a lot like Rue: sarcastic, witty, but a bit more serious than Rue seemed to be. Sarin took out another, larger pouch from their pack, but this time, the contents were edible. They both kicked off their boots, settled against the cave wall, side by side, and ate in silence. Elijah didn't know where they were, or how safe the area really was -- especially at night. The light outside the cave entrance finally died out, leaving only the small fire.

"We can't leave it burning," Sarin said when they'd finished dinner. "This place is relatively well-protected, but there's no sense in risking it."

"Is it safe to sleep?" Elijah asked when Sarin snuffed the fire out with a wave of a hand. Elijah had no clue how the mage did it.

Sarin smirked and spread one of their thin blankets out. Then he lay down, grabbed Elijah's hand, and tugged. Elijah landed on top of the mage. "Whoever said a word about sleep?"

"Only you would think of sex right now."

Sarin rolled them, putting Elijah on bottom, and settled between Elijah's spread thighs. Elijah threaded his fingers through the mage's long hair and took kiss after kiss. Sarin worked a hand between their bodies and cupped Elijah through the thin pants. Elijah groaned softly, rocking into the mage's touch.

"Sarin," Elijah whispered as he thrust against his lover's hand. "Stop teasing and just fuck me already."

Sarin chuckled and rose up enough for them both to undress. Elijah caressed Sarin's chest with both hands and marveled at the soft, furred designs. Sarin gripped one of Elijah's hands and slid it downward. By the time Elijah wrapped his fingers around his lover's cock, Sarin was shaking. The furry designs, Elijah had discovered not long ago, were strong erogenous zones -- almost as much as the hard flesh gliding along his palm, through the tunnel of his fist.

"You're driving me crazy," Sarin growled through gritted teeth.

Elijah kept stroking. He loved the way Sarin moved against him, the power in the mage's body surging. "Let me suck you."

Instead of answering, Sarin pulled away. Elijah grabbed the man's hips and urged Sarin to move higher. Sarin did so, nearly sitting on Elijah's chest. The mage's hard cock pressed against Elijah's lips. Elijah opened and hummed as he sucked the head into his mouth. Sarin hissed and gripped one of Elijah's hands where it rested on Sarin's hip. Elijah sucked and moaned, head bobbing as Sarin rocked back and forth.

"Elijah," Sarin murmured.

Elijah looked up. Sarin's head was back, the mage's eyes closed. The fur seemed to shimmer, even in the dark. Elijah let Sarin slip free. Sarin reached for something, and Elijah prayed it was something slick. Then Sarin moved back down to kneel between Elijah's thighs. Two slippery fingers circled Elijah's hole before pushing slowly inside.

"Yes…" Elijah opened as much as possible, legs spreading more. "God, you're amazing."

Sarin kissed him and added a third finger. "Only my fingers."

"Babe…" Elijah groaned low when Sarin scissored all three fingers. "Fuck. More."

Sarin withdrew and lined up his cock. He sank in deep, not stopping until their bodies touched everywhere. Elijah's head swam in pure bliss. Sex with Sarin went far beyond the physical. Everything the mage did was magical.

When Sarin began moving, Elijah met every stroke and thrust with one of his own. He locked his legs around Sarin's waist, angling his hips so Sarin could go deeper. Nothing else existed anymore. Not the cave, not the darkness, not the cold rock beneath them. Heat flushed through Elijah, filling him every time Sarin moved, in and out.

Elijah wanted it to last forever. His body had other ideas.

Fire shot through him without warning, and Elijah shouted. He bucked upward, driving Sarin deeper, over and over, as he came. Sarin sped up and grunted, more heat pulsing into Elijah in time to their heartbeats.

Chapter Two

They'd left the camp at the break of dawn and continued on for a couple of hours when Elijah spotted the first sign of life besides animals and plants. Several farms loomed in the distance, and beyond them, a wooden wall stood. Farmers on either side of the road stopped and stared, no doubt at the wolf by Elijah's side. He hadn't thought to ask what the locals might think of Sarin. When they reached the gatehouse, the guards warily watched them walk through.

Segorus was smaller than Elijah had expected. He noticed a sign swinging over a doorway, and even though he couldn't make out the words, the mug carved on the fading wood told him exactly what he wanted to know. He led his horse to the tavern and dismounted. After tying the reins to a nearby post, he headed into the building, Sarin on his heels.

Only a few patrons sat around the tables, and all of them fell silent when Sarin curled up at one of the tables near the door. Elijah approached the bar.

"Mighty frightful dog you have," the barkeep said with a nod toward Sarin. "I could use a guard dog like that."

"He's not for sale." Elijah fished out several coins and set them on the bar. "I need information."

The barkeep glanced at the coins, then at Elijah. "I'm your man."

"I'm looking for work, bounties."

"You a bounty hunter then?"

"Let's just say I'm a traveler aiming to make my presence known -- and my skills invaluable -- to the crown."

The barkeep nodded. "King Mirov has many

enemies. I'm sure he'll pay handsomely for their deaths. Outside Segorus, head toward Ethur Mountains. There's a group of wizards hiding in the caves. The king wants them all dead and ten of their medallions as proof of the deed."

"Much appreciated," Elijah said. He snapped his fingers and left the tavern. Sarin followed.

Outside, he untied the reins and climbed back into the saddle. Then he led the way back out of the town. He ignored the guards and the farms, and headed south, toward the mountains that towered over Segorus. As soon as they were out of sight, he stopped. Sarin shifted into human form.

"I know the caves he's talking about," Sarin said. "They run through the mountains. The most habitable section is near here. We have to be cautious. Mirov's distaste for magic has put all magic users on high alert."

"Do you know anything about this group we're supposed to kill?"

"Rogue cults spring up all the time. None of them are friendly."

"Well, that at least makes me feel a little better about slaughtering them," Elijah muttered.

Sarin rested a hand on Elijah's thigh and looked up at him. "I know this isn't something you necessarily want to do, but if we're to make this ruse convincing, we have to do it."

Elijah sighed. "I know. I just --"

A twig snapped and both of them stared into the brush to their left. If they were being watched, it explained why Sarin didn't shift again. The last thing they needed was to let anyone see they weren't ordinary hunters.

Sarin drew his sword from where it lay sheathed

behind Elijah on the saddle. "Show yourself," he called out.

Leaves rustled, then a figure emerged. The young man held his arms up, away from the short sword on his hip and the bow across his torso.

"I am Braden," the man said. "A simple hunter like yourselves, though... perhaps a bit simpler."

Sarin sheathed his sword. "Why were you following us?"

"I wasn't. I am scouting for... Well, let's just say that my employers are not entirely happy with the king."

Sarin glanced up at Elijah, then back to Braden. "Neither are ours."

Braden bowed to them. "Then consider me an ally, for what it's worth."

"We can't stay here," Sarin said. "We're too close to the town. You may travel with us, though rest assured that you will not survive should you attempt anything untoward."

Braden smirked. "I don't know who or what you are, but I've seen enough to know I would stand no chance against you."

Elijah kept silent. He didn't know this world -- and certainly not Braden -- enough to know who to confide in beyond Sarin and their group. Sarin shifted once more, and Elijah noticed Braden watching with interest.

They continued into the mountains, Braden taking the lead. Elijah had the feeling it was more due to not wanting to anger Sarin than anything else. When they neared a cave opening, Braden stopped and found a secluded spot under a small overhang within sight of the cave entrance.

"I came out here to search for sympathizers,"

Braden said. "I can't say much lest I endanger the ones I work for, but we oppose Mirov at every turn. Needless to say, he isn't fond of us, though he doesn't know our identities."

Elijah finally spoke up. "For much the same reason, I can't go into details either. My partner and I are here undercover, so to speak. We hope to gain Mirov's attention as bounty hunters."

"That explains why you're after the group in the caves," Braden said. "I'd hoped to seek them as allies, but from reports I gathered in Segorus, they've gone rogue and will kill anyone."

"Then help us clear them out," Elijah said, "and we'll split the bounty."

"You have a deal, my friend."

"I'm Elijah." Elijah extended a hand, which Braden shook. "And my partner is Sarin."

"It's a pleasure to meet others who have no love for Mirov."

"Likewise," Elijah said. "Now... what do you know of this group?"

"Necromancers, if the rumors in Segorus are to be believed. I'd hoped that wouldn't be the case, that they were simply on the run." Braden scowled. "I care nothing for magic that calls on the dead."

"Neither do we," Elijah said.

"We must be very cautious, however. Surely they know there is a bounty for their deaths, which means they aren't unprepared." Braden drew his sword and nodded at Elijah's bow. "How good a shot are you?"

Elijah readied his bow. "Good enough to not shoot you unless you get in the way."

Braden nodded once. "Works for me. Stay out of sight. Let me and your friend take the lead."

"After you."

The moment they stepped into the cave, Elijah realized why games had not reached the point of Smell-O-Vision. Had he known what to expect, he would never have even considered coming here. The air felt damp and clammy, and it reeked of old dirt, unwashed bodies, and what he prayed weren't rotting things tucked into nooks and crannies.

"You all right?" Braden asked him.

Elijah swallowed down the slight nausea. He couldn't begin to explain why he wasn't used to places like this. He nodded. "You'd think wizards would have a spell or two to zap everything clean."

Sarin let out a canine snort.

"Wait until you venture into a camp of nothing but orcs." Braden made a gagging gesture. "Nasty creatures. Anyway, there are likely to be patrols. If there's one, take him out before he can call for help. Any others, Sarin and I will handle."

Movement down the tunnel alerted them. Braden took cover closest to the approaching patrol, while Elijah crouched farther back, bow ready. Sarin stood between them, fur bristling, entire canine body trembling. Elijah had seen dogs fight, but nothing ever as big as Sarin.

The patrol rounded the turn in the tunnel, made it past the little nook where Braden waited. When no one else followed, Elijah loosed an arrow. The wizard let out a startled gasp before dropping to the cave floor. Blood pooled under his head, the arrow protruding from his neck. Sarin nudged the body until it rolled over. Then he grabbed a large medallion hanging around the corpse's neck and tugged. The rope broke and Sarin brought the medallion to Elijah. Elijah stuffed it into his pack.

"That's one."

"Nine more to go then." Braden peered around the bend, then motioned for Sarin and Elijah to follow.

* * *

By the time they'd cleared the caves of rogue wizards, Elijah had lost all semblance of any appetite. He'd left a lot of the actual slaughter to Sarin and Braden, while he stayed back and fired off arrow after arrow. There had been nearly twenty wizards, though the bounty only called for ten medallions. None of them expressed any interest in being friendly. Not that it surprised Elijah, really. A part of him had come up with the notion that, if he only shot arrows and Braden and Sarin did the majority of the killing, then he wasn't committing murder. If he kept repeating it to himself, Elijah figured he might eventually believe it.

Braden handed him the last medallion. "That's all of them. This sect won't be bothering anyone, at least." He paused for a moment and studied Elijah in silence before continuing. "You are new to this sort of thing, aren't you?"

"I..." Elijah sighed. There wasn't much point lying -- not when he really had no idea what to say. "It's a long story," he said. "The short version is yes... and no. I've hunted animals, but killing people is another thing entirely."

Braden nodded. "I understand. Never forget the first, Elijah. The moment you do, the moment you become numb to taking a life, is the moment you turn into a monster like Mirov. If it helps, this group, according to many rumors, have been causing all sorts of problems for the nearby farms -- including killing. We did the common folk a big favor."

"I hope so," Elijah said. "So now onto Cosei?"

"Yes." Braden led the way back out of the cave.

He'd tied his own roan mare to a tree beside Elijah's horse. He untied both sets of reins and handed Elijah's over. Then he jumped into the saddle. "Have you been to Cosei?"

Elijah climbed onto Shail's back and directed the horse toward the town of Segorus. "Briefly," he lied, unsure how to explain the truth. "Have you?"

"More times than I care to count," Braden replied. "It's a rather large city, overflowing with people, refuse, and trouble. And on top of it all, Mirov sits on a stolen throne."

They left the quiet of the woods and soon reached Segorus. Guards ignored them, for the most part, though a few kept a wary eye on Sarin. Elijah silently thanked God for the mage. With Sarin in wolf form, no one did so much as lift a hand to cause trouble. Elijah and Sarin followed Braden through the narrow, packed street that ran straight through the small border town. People gave them a wide berth, and soon enough, they were heading through the second Segorus gate leading toward Cosei.

Away from the town once more, Braden slowed until he kept pace with Elijah and Sarin. "I'm going to venture a guess that your partner is much more than a shapeshifter."

Elijah glanced at Sarin, who nodded. "In this form, he's just a wolf -- albeit a big one. In human form, though... he is a mage."

Braden stopped abruptly, his horse protesting. "Very few mages share such shapeshifting abilities."

Sarin seemed to look in all directions before shifting into human form. "I am Sarin Eckhert," he said.

Recognition dawned over Braden's face, his expression one of pure awe. "You are the Captain of

Cosei's guard…"

"And a member of the Labyrinthine Order," Sarin added.

Braden bowed in his saddle. "I am honored that you would tell me. I have known a few solitary members of the Order, but their names will remain hidden, as I promised them. I now understand why you are here, though. Do you seek to usurp Mirov?"

Before Elijah could answer, Sarin did. "We seek to return the throne to its rightful owner."

Braden's brows drew together. "I don't understand. Mirov's family has ruled Timiria for ages, he…" His gaze shifted from Sarin to Elijah, then back. "She is alive. The queen is alive?"

Sarin nodded. "Elsbeth lives. We seek to discover what forces Mirov has at his disposal, before we do anything more. He's already sent assassins, though for the traitor he believed her to be. He does not know the woman in our protection is his sister."

"What can I do to aid you?" Braden asked. "I can contact my group, though I swear to not divulge any more information than necessary."

"We need to enter Mirov's service," Elijah said. "I need to find out who is working for him, and what our options are."

Chapter Three

They continued on, making decent time, or at least that's what Elijah thought. He honestly had no way of knowing for sure. Before too much longer, he spotted a few homes and fenced areas further up ahead.

"I can't go near Cosei," Braden said. "The guards know me and will not hesitate to kill me on sight."

"This must have come about after I deserted," Sarin said. "Don't risk yourself getting caught -- or worse. We can get to Cosei and will find a way to contact you once we have any useful information."

Braden nodded. "Be careful. I don't know how long ago you left, but Mirov has a deathgrip on the guard now."

"Thank you." Sarin offered a hand to Braden, who shook it. "Stay safe. We will be in touch."

Braden disappeared into the woods, giving them both a final wave before he was out of sight. Sarin glanced around and shifted back into wolf form. Then he nudged Elijah's horse onward.

The farms weren't very close together, and Elijah didn't see much in the way of protection for them. People stopped working as Elijah and Sarin passed by, though none of them seemed terribly surprised to see such a huge wolf. Elijah wondered if maybe, this far out, people saw much more than city folk did.

Soon enough, the farms were behind them. Elijah let Sarin lead the horse, more or less, and took the chance to get his bearings -- or at least as much as possible. Nothing looked familiar. He hadn't played his character very long, and he'd ventured away from the starting city of Cosei rather early. He honestly didn't remember much of anything.

After several uneventful hours, the sun dropped behind a bank of clouds, and the forests on either side of the dirt road began to creep closer toward it. The road wound through the woods, and Sarin guided Elijah's horse off the path. Elijah gave up trying to figure out where they were going. Sarin knew this place far better.

Sarin stopped in a small clearing and nodded. Elijah led the horse into the middle, then watched as Sarin circled the perimeter several times. It took a few seconds, but Elijah soon noticed a faint glow following Sarin. By the time Sarin returned to Elijah, the clearing's edge shimmered and reflected the trees -- but not Elijah, the horse, or Sarin.

"How did you do that?"

Sarin shifted and offered Elijah a hand down. "I am limited in what I can do while in wolf form, as far as magic goes. This barrier, however, is sufficient. To the untrained eye, there is nothing here."

"You mean we're invisible?" Elijah dropped down and looked around the clearing.

"Yes." Sarin gave him a quick kiss and began removing their packs from the back of the saddle. "It will hold until I dispel it. We are safe. Be aware, however, that once we reach Cosei, I can't promise absolute safety. Despite Mirov's hatred of magic, there are still users in the city. I don't know their allegiances, and it's best to err on the side of caution."

"Good idea."

They both got their blankets spread out and a small fire started. Sarin sat down and Elijah handed him the food pack before joining him. They ate in silence for a few minutes before Elijah spoke up again.

"You said no one can see us," Elijah said. "What

about hearing?"

Sarin glanced up at him and gave him a sexy little smirk. "No, though I'm quite willing to test that theory."

Elijah tossed the last of his bread to the horse, then pushed Sarin backward. He straddled the mage and took a kiss, loving the moan Sarin gave him. He'd never wanted anyone this much, never felt such an urge to touch and taste every single inch. Sarin's hands gripped Elijah's hips, pulling Elijah down harder against his lover's body. Without warning, Sarin flipped them.

"How do you want me, love?" Sarin murmured as he kissed a slow, torturous path along Elijah's neck.

Elijah arched, eyes closing. "In me," he whispered. "Please."

"You will never need to beg me."

Sarin sat up and stripped off his clothing. Elijah managed to do the same. Then Elijah grabbed Sarin's biceps and jerked the man back down. Their cocks rubbed together, precome slicking their skin. Elijah shivered every time Sarin moved. The fur on the mage's thighs drove Elijah absolutely fucking insane.

Elijah groaned when Sarin rocked against him. "Now," he ground out through his teeth.

Sarin chuckled. "As you wish."

Instead of whisking a jar of gel out of thin air, Sarin slid down and shoved Elijah's legs up. Elijah grabbed the backs of his thighs. Hands free, Sarin spread Elijah's cheeks and gave his hole a long, slow, lick.

"Fuck!" Elijah's body jerked, hips lifting for more. "In me, damn it!"

Sarin didn't seem to be in much of a hurry. The mage's tongue pushed into Elijah's body, effectively scrambling what few wits Elijah had left. Elijah moaned Sarin's name, and probably a few other unintelligible words. He didn't know. Hell, he didn't care. Sarin licked and sucked on his skin, tongue plunging in and out of Elijah's puckered hole. The world sort of fell away and nothing else existed but pure fucking bliss.

Sarin finally stopped, but before Elijah could protest, the mage did indeed conjure up something slick. Elijah gave up trying to figure out the man's tricks. His eyes rolled as Sarin's thick cock pushed into his ass. Then, without warning, Sarin began to shift.

"Oh, fuck," Elijah gasped, eyes going wide. He stared up into brilliant blue ones. "Sarin…"

Sarin's human face didn't change much, but the lower half of the mage's anatomy sure as hell did. Elijah's hole stretched around the growing thickness buried inside him until he felt like Sarin would split him open. Then Sarin stopped -- moving, shifting, everything. His gaze never left Elijah's.

Elijah always figured it would hit him like a brick, that he would one day find a guy and the revelation would slam into him. But this… it was quiet, calm, like an epiphany. Everything clicked at one time, within a few breathless seconds.

"Elijah?"

Elijah studied Sarin's face. Then he grabbed Sarin and kissed the man hard. He poured every ounce of emotion he possibly could into that one gesture. Sarin's growl -- something deep, almost triumphant -- rumbled through them both. The world slammed back with a swift thrust of Sarin's hips. Elijah's back bowed, and he cried out into Sarin's mouth, but he didn't let go. Sarin took him over and over, never easing up.

Sarin shoved a hand between their bodies and

gripped Elijah's cock. He pumped it in time to the almost brutal strokes. "I love you," he panted. "I will always love you -- no matter who you are."

"Sarin!" Elijah bucked, spunk shooting over Sarin's fist and onto Elijah's stomach.

Sarin groaned and pounded into him several more times before going still. A low, guttural growl followed, and Elijah felt every minute pulse of the mage's cock as Sarin filled him.

Exhausted, they both collapsed, Sarin half on top of Elijah. Elijah kissed his lover's hair and ran a hand down Sarin's sweat-slick back.

"I love you, too," he whispered.

* * *

Cosei was Tasmorum's biggest city, and it showed. Elijah didn't recall it being so damn crowded, but, then again, he'd only been here in a game. Winding his way through throngs of people, he swiftly began to realize why Sarin deserted. Well, aside from Sarin's true identity as a mage.

Peasants and nobles alike filled the main street and several side streets. Market stalls lined both sides of the main road, and merchants shouted to buyers and passers-by alike. Dogs barked from every single nook and cranny, it seemed, and kids ran all over the place, most of them wilder and louder than the dogs. The nobles generally gravitated toward the farther end of the street, while the peasants stayed closer to the main gate. Houses and buildings towered over everything and everyone, reminding Elijah of some of the poorer places in New York. Beyond it all, though, loomed one of the most imposing places he'd ever seen.

Mirov's palace dominated the entire city below it. Stone walls soared into the air by several stories, and narrow windows were spaced at intervals. The castle's outer wall was built of stone as well, several feet thick, and the gatehouse was enormous. Elijah couldn't stop the shiver as he and Sarin passed under the spiked portcullis gate. One flip of a lever to their right, and they'd both become shish kabobs.

Two guards stepped in front of them.

Elijah forced his heart out of his throat long enough to speak. "I've come regarding the bounty on the cultists' medallions." He held up the bag they'd collected the medallions in with Braden.

One of the guards gave him a curt nod and both men stepped aside. Elijah led his horse to the stable. A groom wandered out, gave Sarin a once-over, then shot a disbelieving look up at Elijah.

"What is he?"

Elijah dismounted and handed the reins to the groom. "My companion," he said. "And my watchdog."

The groom took the reins, hand shaking slightly. "Right. Yes, sir." He backed away very slowly, apparently not keen on turning his back to Sarin.

Elijah bit back a laugh and headed for the main keep, Sarin beside him. If they could pull this ruse off, it would be a miracle. Elijah prayed no one had even the slightest inkling about Sarin's true nature.

Inside, the main hall bustled with nobles, guards, and only God knew who else. Elijah immediately wanted to run the other way. Between his nerves and the knowledge that he and Sarin both would be dead men if anyone discovered the truth, he did his best to not puke.

A man, in fancy clothes, met him halfway to the dais. "Welcome to King Mirov's court. His Highness is not available at this time."

"I've come regarding the bounty on the cultists." Elijah showed the man the bag. "We -- my wolf and I -- cleared the caves. There are no cultists left."

One eyebrow rose and the man took the bag. He peered inside, then nodded. "The king will be very pleased with this news. I am Birin, Steward to King Mirov. I welcome you to Cosei."

Elijah figured bowing was appropriate, so he did. "Elijah, at your service."

Birin's gaze shifted to Sarin. "And your... wolf?"

Fuck! In the insanity of planning this whole thing, Elijah had completely forgotten that Sarin needed a fake name. He blurted out the first name that came to mind. "Liebe. He is called Liebe."

Birin nodded. "Then I welcome you both. I am sure King Mirov will want to thank you personally. Will you be staying at the Red Marquis?"

"I..." Elijah grimaced. "I am afraid I'm rather new to Cosei."

"Ah, I see. The Red Marquis is one of the finest inns in the city. Plenty of opportunities for refreshment and... other, more carnal pursuits, should you wish."

Sarin let out a low, angry growl. Elijah had to bite back another laugh. He rubbed Sarin's head.

"I think I'll find somewhere less... pretentious."

Birin seemed to think for a moment before replying. "We do have a few open rooms, for guests who visit us."

Elijah wasn't sure he wanted to stay in the palace itself, but Sarin discreetly bumped his leg. "That would be perfect, I think."

"Wonderful! Follow me, please."

* * *

Elijah collapsed onto the bed. It was small. Hell,

the whole room was, but he figured it could be much worse. Sarin nudged him. "You'd better have a damn good reason for us staying in here."

Sarin seemed to smile, which was just a tad bit unnerving. When the wolf smiled, every sharp tooth gleamed. Elijah sighed. Sarin didn't do anything without some kind of plan -- that much Elijah had learned. Elijah sat up and looked around the room. Nothing seemed... off. He got up and checked the door, making sure it was locked. When he turned around, he jumped.

"God, Sarin. Don't do that!"

"Sorry." Sarin laughed. "I thought it best if we stay here, in the palace, to watch Mirov. You said you can be sneaky. As soon as we meet Mirov, we will hopefully have a better idea of where to start."

A knock came and, in the blink of an eye, Sarin was a wolf again. Elijah just shook his head and unlocked the door.

"Yes?" he asked the page.

"King Mirov wishes to see you, sir."

"Thank you." Elijah stepped out of the room and Sarin followed. The page made a weird little frightened squeak and nearly ran the other way down the hall. "Well, at least no one will fuck with me."

The room they had wasn't far from the main hall. Elijah found the way and waited until another page -- this one apparently unafraid of Sarin -- announced him. Then the page waved Elijah and Sarin into the hall.

Mirov looked just like his picture on the game box: muscular, bearded, untrusting, and quite haggard. It was amazing that such a man could be related to the beautiful Elsbeth. Mirov motioned for Elijah to approach the dais. Elijah bowed low.

"So you're the one responsible for ridding the countryside of those irritating cultists," Mirov said. "I'd honestly expected someone more..." The king grimaced. "Well, suffice it to say, you are not what I expected. Tell me your name."

"Elijah, Your Highness." Elijah stroked the fur between Sarin's pointed ears. "And this is Liebe, my companion."

"A fine companion he is, too," Mirov said. "I doubt you encounter much trouble with him about."

"Yes, Your Highness. We've been together for years," Elijah lied, though it didn't feel like a lie. "We would like to offer our services to the crown."

"And what services might those be, beyond killing wizards?"

"I am an experienced scout. I know these mountains well. I can blend in, become virtually invisible." Elijah lowered his voice slightly, his gaze focused on Mirov's. "I know there are enemies lurking everywhere. I can be your eyes and ears, and, when need be, your executioner."

Mirov sat back and studied Elijah. "You have proven you can handle yourself well against heretics. Now you will prove your abilities with something far more dangerous."

"Anything, Your Highness."

"There is a detestable thorn in my side, a man who has done everything short of storming my keep. He has killed countless guards and bounty hunters. I want his head."

"You need only tell me his name," Elijah said. "I will do the rest."

"Braden Delarraan."

It took every ounce of willpower Elijah possessed to remain standing. His blood turned ice cold, but he nodded once.

"It will be done."

"Then leave me," Mirov commanded. "Do not return until you have that rogue's bleeding head in your hands."

Elijah bowed and backed away. Then he turned and left the throne room. He headed straight out of the keep. His stomach rolled over itself countless times between the keep and the main gate of Cosei. Outside the city, he veered off into the woods. Soon as he felt safe, he fell against a tree and slumped to the ground, ignoring the scratchy bark. Sarin shifted and crouched in front of him.

"We have to do something," Elijah said. "Sarin…"

"I know." Sarin stood and pulled Elijah up with him. "First thing's first: we find Braden before someone else can."

Chapter Four

It took most of the night, but Elijah finally spotted a tiny glimmer of a campfire far back from the road. He prayed it was Braden and not some bandit camp. He really had no desire to fight right now. He approached the campsite slowly, knowing damn well he'd be dead before he ever saw Braden if he spooked the man. Braden sat at the fire, skinning a small animal.

"Unless you intend to die tonight, I suggest you step into the light," Braden announced without looking up.

"It's us." Elijah moved into the firelight, and Sarin followed suit, in human form.

Braden blinked up at them both. "I hadn't expected to see you so soon. To what do I owe the pleasure, my friends?"

"You're being hunted," Sarin said. "Mirov has a bounty on your head."

"I know." Braden continued skinning what Elijah realized was a rabbit. "He's sent many men to their deaths. Somehow, I'm not surprised he decided to test your skills on me."

"What are we going to do?" Elijah asked. "We have to make this whole thing work, but he wants your head as proof."

Braden looked up, but not at Elijah. He stared at Sarin. "So we give it to him."

"What?" Elijah nearly jumped up, but Sarin caught his hand.

"Magic," Sarin said. "I can cast the same glamour my father used on you. We just need a head to do it on."

Elijah's stomach turned somersaults again.

"Ugh."

"There's a bandit camp not far from here," Braden said. "I caught a glimpse of them before coming here. We kill them all, take one of their heads."

"Why do I get the feeling you've done the head-chopping thing before?" Elijah muttered.

Braden shrugged. "As a fellow bounty hunter, I can't imagine."

* * *

For the thousandth time, Elijah wanted to ask if they really had to do this. He and Sarin had followed Braden to the bandit camp. Now they had to wait.

"We have to kill them all," Braden whispered. "If even one manages to escape, this whole idea is forfeit. I counted seven when I saw them earlier."

Elijah did the same thing and came up with six. "One is missing."

"The seventh is standing watch," Sarin said, returning and shifting into human form again. He'd prowled the perimeter, doing his own brand of scouting. "One of us needs to take him out quickly and quietly. Then we converge on the group."

Elijah slipped his bow off. "I can get the guard."

"Don't miss," Braden warned. "If he alerts the others, this will get messy fast."

Messy. Right. Like decapitation was clean.

Elijah snuck back toward the road. The path leading to the bandit camp was nearly overgrown, and he had to be careful not to make a sound. He avoided the bushes and watched where he stepped. When he spotted the guard, he crouched and drew an arrow as silently as possible. The bandit faced the road, back to Elijah. Elijah drew the arrow, then let it go. It thumped into the back of the guard's neck. The body hit the ground with a thud.

One down. Six to go.

Elijah made his way back to Sarin and Braden. Sarin had shifted into wolf form once more. Braden drew two long daggers instead of his sword or bow. Elijah wondered just how many weapons one damn human could carry.

"Now," Braden mouthed.

Before anyone could blink, Braden rushed from cover. Sarin charged into the campsite and leaped onto one of the bandits. Shouts filled the woods. Braden drove both daggers into the back of one bandit, while Sarin tore another bandit to pieces with claws and teeth. Elijah fired arrow after arrow, taking down two more with several shots.

It didn't take long to finish the small group off. Sarin shook his head and blood dripped from the wolf's teeth. Elijah shouldered his bow and joined Sarin. Braden dragged one of the bandits over to them, then dropped the corpse at Sarin's feet. Sarin shifted into human form.

"How long will the glamour last?" Braden asked him.

"The stronger I make it, the longer it stays. But it will weaken me."

Elijah nodded. "We'll stand guard. How do we..." He gestured to the corpse. "How do we take off the head? A sword isn't going to do it."

Sarin motioned to the body. "Elijah, grab the feet. Braden, sit on the chest."

Elijah wasn't sure he wanted to know what Sarin had in mind. He held onto the bandit's feet, and Braden straddled the dead man's chest. Sarin shifted again, got a mouthful of dirty hair, and, with a vicious snap of his head, ripped the bandit's head clear off the shoulders. Elijah just stared, mouth hanging open. Braden didn't seem to be the least bit unnerved.

"I could have used you a few times on hunts," Braden said as he stood.

Sarin dropped the head. He nosed it until it rolled face-up. Then he resumed human form. "I need silence."

Much like Rue had done, Sarin lifted his hands and closed his eyes. He chanted under his breath, words Elijah didn't recognize flowing nonstop. The bandit's appearance slowly transformed, taking on Braden's looks. The results were uncanny. When done, Sarin sank to his knees. Elijah caught him and let Sarin lean.

"Nice work," Braden commented. "Get some rest. I'll take first watch."

Elijah led Sarin away from the carnage they'd made. Then he helped Sarin lie down. "You okay?"

"I will be," Sarin said. "It takes a good bit of energy, even more so from someone like me. My father is older and far stronger."

"Don't sell yourself short, babe." Elijah sat down against a tree. Sarin rested, head on Elijah's lap. "Try to recuperate."

Sarin drifted off to sleep, and Elijah kept watch. He could see Braden from where they sat. The man hadn't blinked an eye when Sarin used magic. Elijah wasn't sure why he'd expected Braden to, anyway. Mirov had a problem with magic, but from what Elijah had seen so far, most people didn't seem to really care either way.

Elijah closed his eyes to block out the sight of lumps of flesh that used to be human beings. If he didn't see them, then maybe he'd eventually believe the little voice still struggling to hold onto some semblance of innocence.

* * *

"Elijah."

"Hm?" Elijah blinked his eyes open. "Oh, man. Did I fall asleep?"

"You speak strangely for someone of this world."

Elijah met Braden's gaze. "We've come this far, and you support the queen."

Braden nodded.

"Have you ever encountered... travelers? Not your normal, everyday people, but people who don't really belong here."

"I wondered if perhaps there was more to you than meets the eye," Braden said. "I've heard about people like you, though you're the first I've met."

"How I got here is a long story," Elijah explained. "But the more time I spend here -- especially with Sarin -- the more I realize I may very well belong here after all."

Braden glanced at Sarin, who still slept. "You're far more than companions."

"Depends on your definition of companion," Elijah said.

Braden smiled. "Lovers then."

"Another little tidbit to the story, but yes, we are."

"I envy you," Braden said. He sighed and stood. "Up now. You need to get back to Mirov."

Elijah nudged Sarin awake. "Time to go, babe."

Sarin sat up. "I'll be happy when this whole mess is over."

"Tell me about it." Elijah got to his feet and helped Sarin stand. "At least we managed this part. Maybe it'll get us into Mirov's inner circle."

"I'll stay out of sight," Braden said. "I don't know where I'll go, but rest assured, we will meet again. I owe you both a debt I can't repay."

Elijah shook Braden's hand, and Sarin did the same. "You don't owe us anything, but if you're willing, go to Pelarum. The rest of our group is there."

"I will do that then." Braden left them, heading off into the woods.

"Time to see if our little hunt paid off," Elijah said.

* * *

"My champion returns!" Mirov leaned forward in his throne, eyes gleaming with interest. "Is it done?"

Elijah dropped the sack onto the floor of the great hall. "It is."

Mirov gestured for one of his guards to retrieve the sack. The guard opened it and several people around them gasped and whispered when the man pulled out a severed head. Mirov stood and descended the dais steps. He spat on the head, then ushered the guard away.

"You have done me a great service," Mirov announced. "My steward will see that you are properly rewarded."

Elijah bowed. "Thank you, Your Highness."

"You have proven your loyalty. I have another matter -- one that I will trust to no one else." Mirov motioned for Elijah to follow him. The king led Elijah down a hallway and stopped at a closed door. He opened it and waved Elijah inside. Then he shut it, giving them privacy. "I've recently learned of a threat far greater than a single man. There are rumors that the former queen is not dead, as I'd been led to believe."

"What do you wish me to do?" Elijah asked.

"There is a temple half a day's ride from Cosei. A shrine dedicated to the heathen goddess Laenasse. The former queen's royal guards are her acolytes. Find the shrine, and you will find evidence. Of this, I have no doubt. Kill anyone who gets in your way. Defile the temple. The acolytes will not tolerate it. Subdue one of them and bring him to my dungeon. Together, we will learn the truth."

* * *

Elijah sat on the edge of the bed and sighed. How the hell were they going to pull this off? Killing the bandits to steal a head was one thing. Killing mages in Sarin's order was another matter entirely. Elijah knew damn well he couldn't bring one of the mages back here, but if he didn't, the entire plan was shot to hell. He groaned and fell backward.

"We'll figure something out."

"I have no clue what," Elijah muttered. "I'm not going to kill anybody in your order, Sarin."

"We won't." Sarin sat on the bed beside him. They had to be as quiet as possible. "The temple isn't guarded. Acolytes aren't there all the time."

"We have to bring one of them back," Elijah reminded him. "God only knows what sort of torture Mirov plans."

"Priests of Laenasse are drawn to her temples through the spirit," Sarin said. "But proximity to one also grants us a great amount of strength."

Elijah peered over at his lover. "I don't follow."

"Use me as your captive."

"What?" Elijah shot up and scowled at Sarin. "Have you lost your fucking mind? Mirov plans to torture you!"

Sarin rested a hand on Elijah's shoulder. "Just

hear me out, love. I can draw enough power from the temple to sustain me through a great deal of torture. If I have an effigy of Laenasse with me, Mirov and his torturers won't be able to harm me."

"And this helps us... how?"

"It will give him pause," Sarin said. "Make him realize we are not to be trifled with, but it also protects Elsbeth. My heritage grants me more power than many of my fellow priests. I won't break."

Elijah narrowed his gaze. "What aren't you telling me? What is it about you -- and Rue -- that make you two so damn special in the order, beyond Rue being a seer?"

Sarin sighed. "I am descended from the first priests of Laenasse," he said. "Our ancestor -- the first one, was Laenasse's consort."

Elijah felt a rush of something he couldn't begin to name. "Are you telling me that your family is descended from a deity?"

"In a sense... yes."

Elijah blew out a breath. "Who else knows this?"

"Just those in the order," Sarin said. "Raig would claim we are akin to royalty."

"So would I."

Sarin shook his head. "We are not. We are not gods, Elijah. My ancestor -- Laenasse's consort -- was human. She granted him the lupine powers we all now possess. Anyone initiated into the order gains the powers, provided he -- or she -- proves devout."

"This still isn't making me feel good about your insane idea of playing captive."

"It will be fine," Sarin said. "I will be fine."

"Doesn't mean I have to like it," Elijah grumbled, crossing his arms.

Sarin smiled and kissed him, easing Elijah back

onto the bed. "So let me do something you *will* like…"

Elijah gave in. Not like he had much choice -- or willpower to resist. Sarin exuded power and sex appeal, and Elijah prayed the mage's goddess protected them both. For now, though, he let Sarin do what the mage did best.

Sarin licked Elijah's lips, breath warming them. Elijah somehow managed to wiggle out of his pants, while Sarin did the same. Then Sarin straddled him. Elijah dug his fingers into the mage's hips when Sarin ground down onto him. Elijah's cock nestled between the cheeks of Sarin's ass, head barely touching Sarin's sac whenever they moved together.

"You're driving me insane," Elijah murmured in between kisses.

"You expect anything less?"

Elijah snorted. "No." He gripped Sarin's cheeks and spread them apart. Bracing his feet on the bed, he rubbed his cock up and down the crease of Sarin's ass. "Please tell me you can conjure up something."

"Mmhmm…" Sarin kissed Elijah's jaw, neck, then up to Elijah's ear. "Fuck me."

"Slick," Elijah growled. "Now."

Sarin reached out, to where Elijah had no idea, and tapped Elijah's shoulder with something. Elijah took the small vial and shook his head.

"How the hell do you do that?"

"What?"

"Make this stuff appear out of thin air."

Sarin smirked. "I set it on the bed when you were distracted."

"Ass." Elijah slicked up three fingers and rubbed them over Sarin's tight hole. Sarin moaned and rocked back, driving all three fingers deep inside. "Eager, aren't we?"

Nodding, Sarin fucked himself on Elijah's fingers. "I need it," he said, breathless. "Now."

Elijah pulled his fingers out and replaced them with his cock. He grabbed Sarin's hips and jerked downward while thrusting up. Sarin shouted and rose up. The mage rocked and ground onto Elijah, every stroke driving them both closer to the edge. Elijah anchored his feet on the bed again and slammed into Sarin, turning his lover into a panting, writhing, half-shifted mess.

Sarin's cock thickened and lengthened. The mage's fingers wrapped around the shaft and Sarin began stroking it. "Harder," he panted. He fell forward, free hand braced on the bed by Elijah's head. Wild blue eyes stared down into Elijah's. "I love you."

"Yes!" Elijah jerked and thrust in deep. He pinned Sarin down and pumped the mage full of come. Heat splashed onto Elijah's chest and stomach, and Sarin's low growl sent a shiver through Elijah's body.

If the goddess Laenasse didn't protect Sarin, Elijah swore he'd raze the heavens themselves.

"Trust me," Sarin whispered after several moments. He rested his head on Elijah's shoulder.

"I do." Elijah kissed his lover's hair. "I do."

Resurrection Point (DungeonCrawl 4)

Mychael Black

Elijah Burrows and his lover, Sarin Eckhert, are off to do the unthinkable: defile a shrine to Laenasse -- the lupine goddess of Sarin's order. Sarin believes Laenasse will protect him, and Elijah prays the mage is right. But it may take a lot more to protect them both when Mirov discovers the truth.

With war looming over their heads, and a king hellbent on destroying all of Sarin's kind, Elijah is forced to make decisions that no man should ever have to make.

Chapter One

"I can't believe I agreed to this."

Elijah Burrows glared at his lupine lover, but Sarin Eckhart dutifully ignored him. They'd left King Mirov's palace two hours ago. The uneasy sensation in Elijah's gut had only grown stronger, despite Sarin's reassurances they'd be fine. Mirov wanted them to defile the nearby Shrine of Laenasse and capture one of the priests for torture. The whole idea made Elijah want to throw up.

Sarin, in wolf form for now, just chuffed and continued walking through the forest. They'd argued about this insane plan several times since Mirov had tasked it to them. Elijah trusted his lover, but there was no way in hell he was going to do what Sarin asked this time.

"Good thing about you being in wolf form is that you can't fucking argue."

Sarin let out a low warning growl.

Elijah snorted. "From anyone -- anything else -- that might be scary. From you, not so much."

Sarin stopped, looked around, then shifted. He shoved Elijah against the nearest tree. Elijah half expected it. He did not, however, expect the kiss. All protests, all doubts flew from his mind the moment Sarin's lips touched his own.

"I love you," Sarin whispered.

"Likewise." Elijah threaded his fingers through Sarin's long black hair and put a few inches between their faces in order to see his lover's eyes. "That doesn't mean I like this."

"I know, love," Sarin said. "But please trust me. I know my limits. I have faith in Laenasse. She will guard me and protect me. There is nothing Mirov can do to hurt me, Elijah."

Elijah seriously doubted that. Mirov had proven to be one of the most twisted assholes Elijah had ever met. Elijah didn't put anything past the man, especially when it came to magic and the priests of the lupine goddess, Laenasse. Sarin's order bore no love for the king, either. Sighing, Elijah rested his forehead to Sarin's, eyes closed.

"I know you fear for my safety," Sarin murmured. "I would do the same were you in my place."

"How can you be so sure Laenasse's power will protect you? What happens if it doesn't work?" Elijah opened his eyes and stared into Sarin's. "I can't lose you."

Sarin smiled and tipped Elijah's head for another soft kiss. "I know," he whispered, the words breathed across Elijah's lips. "But I have faith -- in Laenasse... and in you."

Elijah wanted to believe Sarin. He really did. Before he could reply, however, a twig snapped to their left. They both froze. It could have been an animal, or even Braden. Elijah prayed for either one, because if someone from Mirov's court spotted them, the entire plan flew out the window -- and their lives would be in even more danger than before. Sarin pressed a fingertip to his lips, signaling Elijah to be silent. Elijah nodded.

In the blink of an eye, Sarin went from fully human to half-man, half-wolf. He spun around and let loose a low, menacing growl. "Show yourself. I see the heat of your body. You will never escape."

The sound sent a shiver through Elijah. He'd seen Sarin fight as a man, and he'd seen Sarin fight as a full wolf. But this was different. In this half-shifted form, Sarin looked more primal, more feral than anything Elijah had ever seen. And he looked hot as hell.

Another twig snapped, and brush rustled. A moment later, a young man Elijah recognized from Mirov's palace stepped out into the open. Shaking from head to toe, the man resembled a servant more than a soldier.

Sarin stalked over and sniffed the man. His lips curled up in a snarl, revealing a mouth full of glistening, razor-sharp teeth. "You reek of fear. You are no warrior."

"N-no, sir," the man stuttered.

Elijah stepped forward. "Who are you then?"

The man swallowed and finally seemed to tear his gaze from Sarin. "N-Nathan. I am no soldier. I work -- worked -- in the king's stables and palace."

"Why are you following us?" Elijah asked. He motioned toward Sarin with a single nod. "Not exactly smart, if you ask me."

"I-I wasn't... I mean..." Nathan sighed and closed his eyes. He breathed deeply for a moment before continuing. "I didn't mean to spy or sneak," he said, opening his eyes to look at Elijah, though not the wolf-man towering over him. "I don't serve the king by choice. When I heard the king tell you to go to the shrine, I had to find a way to stop you. I didn't want you to destroy it." He shot Sarin a quick, nervous glance. "But I guess that's not your intention."

"You said you don't serve by choice," Sarin said. Nathan nodded. "Then whom do you serve?"

For the first time, Nathan really met Sarin's gaze. "His sister -- Queen Elsbeth."

"You know we can't let you return to the

palace," Elijah said. "As much for your safety as ours."

"I can help you," Nathan offered, turning his attention back to Elijah. "I know how to get to the shrine."

"So does he," Elijah said, motioning toward Sarin.

"Please... I'll do anything," Nathan pleaded. "I can't go back there, but I don't... want to die here either."

Sarin snorted. "We aren't going to kill you."

Elijah let out the breath he'd held. A part of him worried Sarin would outright kill the poor man. Sarin wasn't violent, but when even a small portion of the wolf emerged, gentle didn't enter into the equation. Instead of taking bites out of a terrified serving boy, Sarin took a couple of steps back.

"You're not... going to eat me, are you?"

Sarin shrugged. "If I did, what sort of fun would it be for the wolf? He prefers a good chase and hunt."

Nathan blinked. "You can't be serious."

Elijah barely managed to stifle a snicker.

Nathan sighed. "Look. Let me help you. I can't go back there. My family was free until Mirov stole the throne from the queen. Then he enslaved most of the peasants in Cosei and the surrounding towns. He keeps watch through his guards in the other cities, but here..." Nathan shook his head. "If you do something Mirov doesn't like, if you set as much as a single toe out of line..." Nathan drew a finger across his throat.

Elijah shuddered.

"So Mirov outright kills indiscriminately," Sarin said.

"How can he keep doing that?" Elijah asked. "Wouldn't the people eventually just revolt?"

"Not if they're too scared," Sarin pointed out. He

lifted a clawed hand, and a blue flame flared to life in his palm.

Nathan grabbed Sarin's arm and jerked it down. "Don't *do* that!" He shot a quick glance around, then scowled at Sarin. "Mirov has eyes everywhere. If anyone sees so much as a hint of magic, you're a dead man."

Sarin smirked, though it resembled a half-snarl. Then he shifted back to human. "I already am."

"Oh, gods..." Nathan shook his head. "You're... you're the captain of Cosei's guard."

"I was," Sarin corrected. "Needless to say, I no longer am."

* * *

Sarin led them to a cave nestled into the side of a nearby mountain. He disappeared into the darkness, then summoned a blue flame. "This way." He'd remained in human form, though Elijah had the feeling it was primarily for Nathan's benefit.

"How far is the shrine from the entrance?" Elijah asked him.

"Not too deep inside. Most of Laenasse's actual shrines are in caves -- reminiscent of the elusive nature of wolves," Sarin explained. "When she granted her consort -- the first priest -- with the lupine gift, she instructed that her shrines be hidden from others. Only the truly devoted are able to find it. The layman shrines are the only ones in the open. Few of them still exist due to Mirov."

Elijah glanced back over his shoulder at Nathan. "So what are your plans once we find the shrine? You know our orders."

"Are you really going to destroy it?" Nathan asked.

"No." Sarin stopped and turned to face them both. "Mirov wants a priest to torture for information. We're going to give the bastard one."

"But…" Nathan's eyes narrowed. "You're talking about yourself, aren't you?" Sarin nodded. "Mirov will kill you!"

Elijah wanted to echo that statement, but he kept his mouth shut. He trusted Sarin.

"When we reach the shrine, I will draw on Laenasse's power. She will protect me from anything Mirov can dish out."

Nathan didn't look convinced. "And if she doesn't?"

"She will."

Elijah sighed and just shook his head when Nathan tried to argue. "Don't bother. His mind is made up."

Sarin turned and continued down the narrow passage. Soon the rough stone beneath their feet became chiseled steps. Elijah counted nearly twenty before Sarin stopped once more.

The cavern opened up, and on the far side stood a rock altar. A statue of a naked woman with two wolves at her feet towered over it. Gay or not, Elijah couldn't deny her beauty. On the altar sat a single goblet and a short knife. Sarin stripped down and knelt. Head bowed, he took several deep breaths before shifting into his half-form.

"My Lady," he murmured, "I come to you, as your humble servant, and ask for your protection. My people are in danger. Our queen must regain her throne. To that end, I must find out what Mirov knows. I offer myself, my life, in exchange for your power."

Sarin picked up the knife and drew it across his palm. Elijah swallowed when the blood welled up in

Sarin's hand. Blood, as a general rule, didn't bother Elijah. But when the blood belonged to his lover...

"My life," Sarin said, holding his hand over the goblet, "for your protection."

The blood dribbled into the goblet. Sarin pulled his hand back, and Elijah watched in fascination as the wound healed on its own. Before he could really think too much on it, Sarin began to glow. A blue shimmer surrounded Sarin's body, and a tendril snaked from his torso to the statue. Rock creaked and pebbles tumbled to the floor of the cave. Elijah and Nathan stumbled backward when the statue's eyes opened.

"My beloved Sarin... my grandson..."

The world sort of tilted. Elijah fell back against the nearest cave wall and slid to the floor. He had not just hear what he thought he heard. Had he?

"Yes, my Lady," Sarin replied.

The statue -- Laenasse -- smiled. It looked bizarre, like an image projected perfectly onto the rock itself. "You give much to aid your brethren. You shall have my strength. Reveal nothing, and know that you have my love." The statue made eye contact with Elijah. "And my blessing."

"Thank you, my Lady," Sarin answered.

The statue returned to normal. Sarin stood, albeit a bit shaky. Elijah went to help steady him. "Why the hell did you not tell me?" Elijah muttered.

"What? That my grandfather was the first?" Sarin sighed. "I told you he was an ancestor."

"Yeah, though I'd say he was a bit more than that," Elijah grumbled. "God, Sarin. You're the grandson of a fucking god. How the hell are you not one? Even a demi-god."

They headed back over to the wall where Nathan stood plastered against the stone, his eyes wide. Elijah couldn't really blame the man.

"Because my ancestor -- my grandfather -- was mortal," Sarin replied. "A human. He was not a god, and neither are his descendants."

Elijah helped Sarin lean back on the wall. "So what about the other priests? Well, the ones before Mirov waged war on your order. Are you all related?"

Sarin shook his head. "No. Anyone with enough devotion and a true spirit can become a priest of Laenasse. Only those of us who are directly descended from the consort, however, possess enough power to oppose someone like Mirov. Even then, we must do what I have done."

"What *did* you do?" Nathan asked, breaking his stunned silence.

"I asked for her strength. She gave it." Sarin glanced at Elijah. "Behind the statue is a niche in the rock. There are extra priest robes there. I need one if Mirov is to believe I am merely a priest."

"How about your appearance?" Elijah asked. "Won't he recognize his own captain?"

"That's unavoidable. It will certainly give him pause when he discovers we are everywhere."

Elijah scowled at his lover. "Or it may piss him off so fucking much that not even Laenasse can protect y-"

A kiss silenced him. He wanted to shove Sarin away, but instead, he fisted both hands in the man's hair and refused to let go. Sarin broke the kiss but didn't pull away. Forehead against Elijah's, Sarin stared into Elijah's eyes.

"I love you," the mage whispered.

"And I love you. Which is precisely why I'm so fucking terrified."

"I know, love," Sarin said. "All I can ask is that

you trust me."

Elijah sighed and released Sarin. "I do."

"So…" Nathan looked quite uncomfortable for a moment. "What's next?"

Elijah stepped back a little. "Good question, though I think we should take a rest while we can. Sarin will need every bit of energy for when we get back to the palace."

Sarin nodded. "That I will."

"All right." Nathan pushed away from the wall. "I think I might go… explore, or something."

Elijah smiled. Nathan didn't strike him as being any sort of bigot. The poor man simply appeared to be a tad confused. Then it hit him. When Nathan wandered off, Elijah just shook his head.

"What?"

"He's in the closet."

"Closet?" Sarin asked, sliding down to the floor. He held out a hand to Elijah.

Elijah straddled his still-naked lover. "It means he's gay -- like us. But, for whatever reason, either he hasn't fully admitted it to himself, or he doesn't want anyone else to know."

"Ah."

Hands on Elijah's hips, Sarin pinned Elijah down. Hardness pressed up against Elijah's ass, making him wish he was nude as his lover. But it couldn't stop him from doing something else. He gave Sarin's a lips a quick kiss, then shimmied down between the mage's furry legs. He gripped Sarin's thick cock and swiped his tongue over the leaking tip.

Sarin hissed and gripped Elijah's hair. "Love."

Elijah swallowed him down, inch by inch. Sarin moaned Elijah's name, the sound morphing into a feral growl when Elijah cupped the heavy sac and gave it a gentle squeeze. Sticky droplets coated Elijah's tongue as he came back up to the tip. He sucked on it, earning another growl from his lupine lover. Sarin's thighs hardened, the muscles flexing. Elijah began bobbing up and down, working one hand on Sarin's balls while the other slid up to trace the blue furred designs on Sarin's torso. Sarin sucked in a sharp breath and thrust into Elijah's mouth.

Elijah had learned early on that the patterns of fur were also highly sensitive. He loved toying with them, every stroke of his fingers driving Sarin absolutely insane. Before long, Sarin's thrusts quickened. Elijah tugged on the mage's balls once.

Sarin let out a roar that echoed through the cavern. Hot spunk shot over Elijah's tongue and down his throat. He swallowed every precious drop before licking Sarin clean.

"You really... should do that... more often," Sarin panted.

Elijah chuckled and rose up for a kiss. Sarin's moan filled his mouth. "Hell yes."

Chapter Two

The trip back to the palace could've taken forever as far as Elijah was concerned. Sarin, wearing a priest's hooded white robe with blue trim, walked behind Elijah, wrists bound by a rope. Elijah held the other end. Nathan had found a camp of travelers soon after they'd left the cave. Elijah figured it was the safest place. Certainly safer than where he currently led his bound lover.

Guards at the city's gate stepped aside, unable to hide their surprise. Elijah ignored them, along with the peasants who lined the streets to gawk, and made his way to the palace. When he reached the doors of the main hall, the massive things swung open. Saying a silent prayer to whatever god or goddess listened, Elijah stepped into the great hall.

Mirov sat on his throne, talking to several men Elijah assumed were advisors of some sort. The moment Elijah walked in, however, everyone fell silent. Mirov's gaze landed on Sarin. The king's twisted smile made Elijah want to throw up.

"I must admit, I did not think you capable of this." Mirov motioned for Elijah to approach the dais. He held out a hand.

It took a few seconds for Elijah to realize Mirov wanted the rope. He reluctantly handed it over. "The priest fought hard," Elijah said. "What are your plans for him?"

Mirov smirked, fisted the rope in his hand, and jerked. "Oh, I'm sure I can think of many things to do with this wretched --"

Sarin stumbled forward and his hood fell back. Gasps resounded around the room. Mirov's face turned deep red.

"You!" The king shot to his feet and shoved Sarin backward.

Sarin landed hard on the floor in front of Elijah. "You can never find all of us," Sarin said as he stood. "My brethren are everywhere."

"Seize him!"

Guards swarmed Sarin. Elijah wanted to kill every single one, but they forced him out of the way. After binding Sarin's arms and gagging him with a bit of dirty cloth, they pushed him toward the throne. Mirov stepped down and grabbed Sarin's hair, jerking the mage's head back at a painful angle, if Sarin's wince was anything to go by.

"For your treachery, I will take great joy in tearing you apart," Mirov growled. He let go, then slapped Sarin's face hard. "Take him to the dungeon," Mirov barked.

The guards hauled Sarin away. Elijah stared at their backs, his heart thundering in his chest.

"As for you..." Mirov approached Elijah and smirked. "Your prize." He tossed a heavy coinpurse at Elijah. "And as a bonus, you will witness the priest breaking under my... ministrations."

Unable to even form words, Elijah could only nod. If he opened his mouth... the entire plan would be shot.

"Have you dined?" Mirov asked. He clapped his hands and servants scurried into the room, bearing trays filled with food. "Come. Join me! We will sup, and then we will pick apart every traitorous inch of my *former* guard captain."

Mirov took his place at the head of the largest table. His advisors sat on either side of him. A single place remained empty a few seats down from Mirov.

The thought of food made Elijah queasy. He bowed low.

"Your Highness, I fear I must retire for a while," Elijah lied.

"Ah, I understand. I know my former captain most likely put up quite a fight," Mirov said. He clapped his hands once again, summoning another servant to him. "Please show our guest to his chambers. Ensure he has whatever he needs or desires."

The servant bowed, then approached Elijah. "If you will follow me, my lord."

Grateful to be out of Mirov's vile presence, Elijah nodded. "After you."

He followed the servant out of the throne room and down a long corridor. They started up a set of stairs, then stopped at a wooden door. The servant opened it and stepped back before handing an ancient-looking metal key to Elijah.

"There is a rope at the head of the bed," the servant said. "Should you need anything at all, pull the rope and a servant will be with you."

"Thank you."

Elijah walked into the room and looked around. It wasn't sparse, but it wasn't opulent, either. The canopied bed dominated the room, its drapes and bedding a deep shade of blue that reminded Elijah of Sarin's fur. Elijah glanced toward the door. The servant was gone.

After hiding the coinpurse under the bed and setting his bow on the bed, Elijah snuck out of the room. He inched his way down the steps and out into the corridor. Other doors lined both sides, and light flickered from behind one of them. Although his bow was out of the question in such tight quarters, Elijah still had his dagger. He drew it and headed for the door with the light. He glanced around, then opened the door slowly. More steps led to what he prayed was the dungeon. Somewhere down there, Sarin waited.

The farther he went, the brighter the light grew. Sounds echoed up the stairwell -- voices, the unmistakable crack of a whip. Then came the cries of pain. Elijah shuddered and vowed to get Sarin the fuck out... and find a way to free everyone else.

The steps ended at another door, this one banded in iron. Elijah pushed it open and peered around it. Torches flickered along the walls of the large room, illuminating all manner of torture devices the likes of which he'd only seen in horror movies. Elijah swallowed down a surge of fear and nausea. He had to keep it together.

"I believe my poor friend has retired for the evening."

Elijah slipped past the door and into the room. He hid behind what turned out to be an iron maiden. A moment later, the door opened and Mirov strolled in like he was head of a lavish parade. Elijah rolled his eyes.

"Oh, well," Mirov said to the four guards behind him. "I suppose he shall have to miss the fun."

One of the cell doors swung open and two more guards hauled a robed man in shackles out. Elijah covered his mouth to stifle the gasp.

"I trusted you," Mirov said as he walked around Sarin. The mage remained silent, staring straight ahead. Mirov grabbed Sarin's hair and jerked. "And this is how you repay me?"

"I have been hers far longer than you have sullied this earth," Sarin said, voice even, without any hint of fear.

Mirov sneered and shoved Sarin toward an X-shaped structure. "Strip him and bind him."

The guards dragged Sarin to the structure, then tore off his robe. He put up no resistance when they tied his ankles and wrists to each beam, leaving him spread-eagle, back to the room. Mirov approached and grabbed something one of the guards handed him. Elijah's eyes widened when the whip unfurled. The tail dragged along the dirty stone floor, its end split into three strands, each one tipped with a curved barb.

Unable to do anything against six guards and Mirov, Elijah watched in horror as Mirov snapped the whip. Sarin jerked and shouted, blood welling along the gashes in his back. Mirov struck again, dragging a scream out of Sarin. Elijah grit his teeth.

"Where are the others?" Mirov demanded.

When Sarin didn't answer, Mirov whipped him again. Sarin cried out, and blood poured down his back. He began to shake as fur covered his lower body.

"Disgusting!" Mirov tossed the whip to the side. Then he lifted a torch from one of the wall sconces. "I know enough about your wretched kind." He started for Sarin, blazing torch in hand. "If the whip does not make you talk, perhaps this will."

Sarin screamed the second the fire touched his furred torso.

"No!"

Elijah rushed from his hiding place, dagger in hand. He ducked and stabbed one guard in the stomach before dodging the sword from another.

"Kill him!" Mirov commanded the other four guards.

The guards all converged on Elijah while Mirov escaped, running out of the dungeon. Wood splintered and a roar filled the room. Sarin broke away completely from the X-shaped structure and shredded the nearest guard with his claws. Elijah spun and caught another one in the ribs with his dagger. The guard doubled over, and one swipe from Sarin's massive paw sent the guard's head rolling across the stone floor.

They both took on the last two guards, though Sarin did the most damage. Alone, dead bodies at their feet, they finally breathed. Sarin dropped to his knees.

"Sarin!"

"I'm fine," Sarin grunted. He shook his head and inhaled deeply. "Just give me a moment."

"I'm not sure we have a moment." Elijah glanced up at the door. "Mirov is probably gathering a fucking army now."

Sarin nodded. "We have to get back to the others."

"What about your-" Elijah ran a hand over Sarin's back. "But... the whip. The cuts."

Sarin moved his hair off of the back of his neck to reveal a tattoo of Laenasse. "She bestowed it upon me at the shrine. Mirov may know some things, but he doesn't know about this."

"Nice trick," Elijah said. He helped Sarin stand. "Are you okay then?"

"Yes."

"How do we get the hell out of here?" Elijah looked around, but nothing besides the cell doors resembled exits. "We can't go out that way."

Sarin started for the cell he'd been in before. "Come on. There's a barred window in here."

Footsteps echoed down the stairwell. Guards shouted.

"Now!"

Elijah hurried after Sarin. He stood back while

Sarin gripped the bars in the window. Sarin shifted into half-form and tore the bars out of the stone. Elijah whistled low.

"Remind me to never piss you off, babe."

Sarin snorted and held out a hand. "Out." At Elijah's glare, Sarin sighed. "I'll be right behind you."

With Sarin's help, Elijah scrambled out. He reached down and gave Sarin a hand up. They ran to the nearest building and hid behind it. Guards rushed into the cell, and Elijah watched as one guard after another scrambled through the battered window casing. Instead of coming toward Elijah and Sarin, however, the guards scattered, going in various directions.

"They'll be searching the city," Sarin whispered. "Our best bet is to wait until nightfall and sneak out."

Elijah glanced up. "It's nearing sunset. Think we can hide long enough?"

"This way."

* * *

"I still don't understand," Elijah said as he and Sarin made their way through the forest just outside of Cosei. "I mean, I get why your wounds healed, but the fire seemed to do more damage than the whip."

"You know the fur is patterned. Well, those patterns are not random." Sarin held up a hand when they neared a clearing. The light of a campfire shone through the trees.

"Maybe it's the camp where we left Nathan," Elijah said.

Sarin nodded. "It is. But... something isn't right." He gestured for Elijah to get down and then he shifted into his full wolf form.

Elijah crouched behind a clump of bushes and

watched. Sarin stalked the perimeter of the clearing, sniffing the ground. Then he moved farther into the clearing itself.

"Elijah!"

Elijah bolted from his hiding place, dagger drawn. He skidded to a stop, barely tripping over a headless body. "Oh, my God…"

Sarin growled low and nosed a body until it rolled over. Elijah picked his way carefully around the corpses. The fire still burned, but Elijah didn't see anyone alive.

"Where's Nathan?" Elijah asked.

Sarin padded over to one of the bodies. When he pushed it over, it groaned. He shifted immediately and knelt by Nathan's side. "Nathan?"

Elijah sheathed his dagger and hurried over. "He's alive!"

"Barely." Sarin brushed Nathan's hair from the young man's dirt-streaked, scratched face.

"Who…" Nathan licked his lips. He blinked his eyes open and sucked in a breath. "Sarin?" He rolled his head to the side. "Elijah?"

"Who did this?" Sarin asked him.

"I don't know," Nathan muttered. "Some of us were eating and talking. Others were sleeping. Cloaked figures came out of the darkness and started slaughtering everyone."

Sarin helped Nathan sit up. "We can't stay here. Mirov knows about me. He's waged war on my order. Elijah and I escaped, but they're after us now."

"Okay." Nathan stood and sighed. "I hurt like hell. Where are we going?"

"Back to Pelarum," Sarin said. "Where the majority of my order are. Do you need to get anything before we head out?"

Nathan scanned the clearing and winced. "Not... really."

Elijah spotted a body with a bow near it. He picked up the bow and checked it over for any damage. Sarin handed him a quiver with arrows tucked inside. Elijah strapped the quiver around his torso, then slung the bow over one shoulder.

"Now I feel better," he said.

Sarin smiled. "Likewise. I prefer you out of the close combat."

Nathan cleared his throat.

Elijah smirked and waved in what he hoped was the general direction of Pelarum. He still had no sense of which way was north in this place.

They set off through the forest again, Sarin in the lead and Elijah in back. Nathan stayed between them since he had no fighting experience. Elijah wanted to ask a million questions, but he figured he'd better wait until they were somewhere safe.

"It will take quite a while to get back to Pelarum," Sarin said. "We will go as far as we can, then find refuge to rest. If we stop only when absolutely necessary, then we should make good time."

Chapter Three

"You're pacing."

Ruelaeri ignored his lover's remark. Sarin and Elijah had been gone for only a few days, but it felt like a lifetime. Rue had no idea if his son would even return. Sarin was strong, but Mirov was twisted and evil. A nagging feeling swirled in Rue's gut. Something had happened. He could feel it.

"Rue."

Strong hands caught Rue. He looked up into Raig's eyes.

"They will be fine."

"You don't know that," Rue argued. "No one does. Not even I, Seer of the Order, can foresee what will happen. What if Mirov doesn't believe the ruse? What if-"

A kiss silenced him.

"I hate it when you do that," Rue muttered on his lover's lips.

Raig chuckled. "You mean kiss you?"

Rue wanted to call the man every foul thing he could think of, but being so close to Raig scrambled his brain. "I am one of the most powerful mages in this damned world, and I can't do so much as think with you around."

Raig grinned and slipped a hand between them. "Good."

Rue's knees threatened to give way when Raig's large hand cupped him through his clothing. Every ounce of resistance vanished. Torn between wanting to beg and wanting to smack the knowing smirk off his lover's face, Rue let Raig lead him down the hall toward their chambers.

Once inside, Raig shut the door and pushed Rue up against it. The warrior's muscled body pinned Rue, every battle-hardened inch igniting an inferno inside that hadn't gone out in decades. Rue gave up trying to ignore it. He threaded his fingers through Raig's long hair and swallowed the man's groan in a kiss.

Strong hands swiftly divested Rue of his clothing. It didn't take long for Raig's clothes to drop to the floor, either. Naked, Rue arched between the wooden door and Raig, head tipped as Raig kissed a path over his neck.

"I don't remember how long it has been," Raig murmured on Rue's overheated skin. "Nor do I care. I will never tire of touching you, my love."

Rue nodded, struck mute. Raig had never been a sentimental man, but every once in a while, he said something that took Rue's breath away. "Please," Rue whispered.

"On the bed."

Raig stepped back and Rue went to the bed. He sprawled out and waited while Raig retrieved the oil. Then Raig crawled between his legs. Rue forced his eyes to remain open the moment two thick fingers, slick with oil, stroked his entrance.

"I could do this forever," Raig whispered. "Just touch you like this, watch the flush crawl up your body."

Rue moaned when both large fingers breached his entrance. Gasping, eyes wide, he stared up at Raig. Nothing else existed except them. Rue wanted to speak, to tell Raig how much he needed it, but words refused to leave his lips. Every stroke of Raig's fingers pushed Rue just a little bit closer to the edge.

"Ready for me?"

At Rue's nod, Raig withdrew and lined the head

of his cock up at Rue's hole. Then unbelievable heat and pressure flooded Rue's body. His lover's cock filled him, stealing what little sanity remained. Rue cried out, fingers clutching Raig's shoulders, digging into the man's skin. Raig's low groan seemed to reverberate through both of their bodies.

"I love you," Raig whispered when he stopped moving, seated fully inside.

"As I love you." Rue exhaled, his body growing accustomed to Raig's girth as if this were the first time. In truth, they'd made love the day before yesterday. "Now show me."

"My pleasure."

Raig began rocking, thrusting and grinding, hips doing the half rotation thing that drove Rue crazy. One big hand pushed between them and gripped Rue's neglected, leaking cock. Rue shouted and bucked, pushing his cock through the tunnel of Raig's huge fist. It didn't take much longer.

The world beyond Rue's line of sight flashed, illuminating the room for the briefest moment. Raig growled and kissed Rue hard, his rhythm growing faster. Dark blue fur started covering Rue's lower body. Raig released Rue's cock and traced a fingertip along the patterns of fur.

"Raig!" Rue bucked, crying out as semen splashed onto his stomach and Raig's.

"Yes…" Raig slammed into him and kissed him. The thick cock buried in Rue pulsed, filling him with heat.

Unable to focus on anything beyond their bed, Rue let his warrior love him into a temporary oblivion.

* * *

Raig had managed to get Rue's mind off of the

situation for a time, but not for long. Back in the great hall, Rue couldn't sit still. He wanted to run into the torrential downpour just outside and scream at the gods to bring Sarin and Elijah home. Sarin was strong, but Rue feared for his safety as any decent father should.

"You knew Sarin would be gone for some time," Raig pointed out.

"Don't remind me."

"Rue, Sarin knows how to defend himself. I daresay Elijah does as well."

"It doesn't help," Rue said. "What if-"

The massive doors of the great hall opened, letting in the cold rain. Three figures strode into the hall -- one of them beloved and familiar. Relief swept through Rue's body.

"My son."

Sarin went right into Rue's arms. "We're safe," he said.

"I was so worried." Rue let himself really breathe for the first time since Sarin and Elijah had left. "I feared Mirov had --" He looked at Sarin, into his son's eyes. "He knows."

Sarin nodded. "I don't know how he discovered our weakness, but he did. When the whip didn't work, Mirov tried to burn the fur off of me."

Rue shuddered. "Are you all right?"

"I am now," Sarin said.

"Tell me all about it. We need to know what he knows." Rue dragged Elijah into a hug. "Thank you," he whispered. "Thank you for protecting my son."

"You're very welcome." Elijah smiled and stepped back. "Rue, Raig, this is Nathan. Nathan, I'd like you to meet Ruelaeri, Seer of the Labyrinthine Order, and his lover, Raig."

Nathan smiled, albeit a bit nervously, and extended a hand. Both men shook it. "Good to meet you. I am no warrior, but I can do a lot of other things. Just tell me what to do. I want to help."

"You look familiar," Rue said. He couldn't place it, but Rue swore he'd seen Nathan before now.

"I have never left Cosei," Nathan said. "My family was forced into servitude, like most of the other peasants in the city."

"I thought we had visitors."

All of them turned to face Queen Elsbeth, though they had yet to actually claim her throne. She neared them, her smile bright and welcoming. In the blink of an eye, however, her smile disappeared, replaced by an expression of utter shock. Aven, Lord of Pelarum, stood behind her, his face an equal mask of disbelief.

Rue followed their gazes straight to Nathan. The similarities stunned him. "May I present... Lord Aven of Pelarum and Queen Elsbeth..." he muttered.

"I..." Elsbeth paled.

Aven caught her in his arms. Raig and Elijah rushed to help him set her gently in one of the thrones. The lord glanced at Nathan, then Rue. "May I speak with you, Rue?"

"Of course, my Lord." Rue nodded for Sarin to escort Nathan to a room. "Sarin, would you please show our new guest where he may rest?"

Rue followed Aven out of the throne room and into a side room. From the open door, they kept an eye on Elsbeth while Raig and Elijah attended to her.

"You saw it."

Rue met Aven's gaze. "I did."

Aven sighed and raked a hand through his hair. "When we -- Elsbeth and I -- first began our relationship, we were young, not even eighteen. She was royalty, and I was a noble. Her parents, while fair people, would not have condoned our courtship."

"I understand," Rue said. "Well, your side of things, anyway. I've never quite understood the concept of standing in the way of love."

Aven smiled slightly. "Thank you."

"But that doesn't explain why Nathan looks so much like you both," Rue said. "Unless…"

Aven sat down on a nearby crate. "When we found out she was pregnant, Elsbeth panicked. She feared her parents would do something horrible to the child, especially since it was out of marriage. She gave birth to a healthy baby boy and left him with the midwife who delivered him, with the assurance that he would be well-cared for."

"Nathan is your son then?"

"He is. We have secretly followed his life, and I had people watching him. We never thought we would see him again."

Rue exhaled. "Does he know this?"

"Unless his adopted parents told him?" Aven shrugged. "I honestly don't know."

* * *

Sarin sighed as he sank down into the hot, steaming water. Even with his eyes closed, though, he knew when his lover neared the tub. He reached out and grabbed Elijah's hand. Then he tugged.

"Damn it!" Elijah laughed. "You ass."

Sarin opened his eyes and smiled. "I love hearing your laughter." He brushed his other hand across Elijah's cheek. "It reminds me why we fight."

"Will you at least let me get my clothes off?"

Sarin chuckled and let go. "Only if you promise to come back."

Elijah got out of the tub and stripped off his soaking wet clothes. Then he stepped back into the water and straddled Sarin's thighs. Hands on Elijah's hips, Sarin held his lover close and opened for a kiss. Elijah hummed and rocked. With a bit of shifting, Sarin situated them both so his cock glided between Elijah's buttocks.

"Fuck me," Elijah murmured.

"My pleasure."

Sarin rose up and held onto Elijah. Elijah's legs locked around him, Sarin walked to the bed and turned. He fell back onto it, Elijah still on top of him. Elijah reached over and grabbed the jar of oil off the bedside table. Then he scooted down a little and dribbled oil over Sarin's cock.

"Elijah…" Sarin growled, hips lifting.

Elijah smiled and stroked, hand pumping Sarin slowly. "Yes?"

"Stop teasing."

Elijah smirked and climbed back on top. Sarin lined up and groaned as Elijah sank down onto his cock, enveloping him in tight, slick heat. Nothing compared to this. Nothing in this world. The transition from Elian to Elijah had been a bit awkward but almost seamless. They were the same person, the same soul in the same body.

"I love you," Elijah whispered, rocking slowly, hips grinding.

Sarin moaned and gripped his lover's short hair. Their disguises had faded, and Elijah once again resembled the man Sarin loved more than life itself. He rolled them and dove into a kiss, drinking in Elijah's moans as he thrust harder, faster. The shift came on fast this time. Elijah's groans turned desperate as Sarin's cock swelled in size.

"Fuck," Elijah panted. "Oh, God. Sarin…"

"I love you," Sarin gasped in Elijah's ear. "So fucking much."

"Yes!" Elijah bucked, heat spurting between their bodies.

Sarin growled and planted his hands on the bed to brace himself. His claws popped into the bedding, the pillows, and the sensation of Elijah's skin against the fur drove Sarin out of his mind. He threw back his head and howled as he came, filling his lover with his own thick heat.

Chapter Four

Elijah listened more than he talked. After a lengthy nap following their lovemaking, he and Sarin had joined Rue, Raig, Aven, and Elsbeth in the throne room to hash out details of what they'd learned. He didn't even want to think about that whole experience. He wondered where Nathan had run off to, seeing as how the young man had pretty much disappeared as soon as they'd arrived.

"So Mirov knows about the symbols," Rue said. He sighed and sat back in his chair. "I can't say I'm surprised."

"He's going to hunt every one of us down." Sarin stood and began pacing. "He knows our weaknesses."

"Can we not contest his rule?" Raig asked. "What if Elsbeth were to announce her presence?"

Aven and Rue seemed to exchange glances. Then Aven stood. "There is... another way."

Nathan wandered into the room, looking like he'd just woken up. "So this is where everyone got off to."

Aven went to Nathan and took the young man's hand, leading him toward the table where they all sat. "I have an announcement, my friends. Elsbeth and I discussed this, and we felt it was time to break our silence." Aven turned and put both hands on Nathan's shoulders. "Welcome home... my son."

Elijah nearly fell out of his chair. Sarin froze and stared at Aven. The only one who didn't seem too surprised was Rue.

"What?" Nathan shot a quick glance around the table, then back to Aven. "My parents were peasants."

Aven smiled, though it seemed a bit sad. "Your

adopted parents were, yes. Your mother and I were young -- and from two very different places in society. Had her parents known... Well, we feared for your life."

Nathan looked like he was going to fall over. "So who is my real mother?" When Elsbeth stood, Nathan swayed a bit. "I..."

Elsbeth opened her arms. It took only a split second before Nathan rushed to her. "I'm so sorry," she whispered. "I love you. I have always loved you."

Nathan nodded and sniffled. "This does explain a few things."

"Like what?" Elsbeth asked.

Nathan stepped back and held up a hand. A blue flame flared to life before he snuffed it out. "I've kept it secret."

Elijah blew out a breath. "So there is an heir to the throne," he said. "Will the people accept Nathan? He has magic, just like Elsbeth. The people knew she did."

"They blindly followed my brother's dictates." Elsbeth led Nathan over to the table where the others sat. "I can't come forward if he still lives. There are still those who support Mirov, no matter how vile he is. My brother has assassins hidden all over the land, those loyal to him to their deaths."

Nathan kept silent, but he appeared thoughtful as he listened. Elijah wondered what went through the young man's head. Finding out you were adopted was bad enough, Elijah figured. Finding out you were royalty... Elijah couldn't begin to imagine how *that* felt.

"I was a lowly servant," Nathan said.

Everyone turned their attention to him.

"My parents were not well known, and I certainly was not. No one knows me."

"He has a point," Rue stated. "The royal bloodline branches in many places. Who is to say a long-lost relative cannot contest the throne?"

Nathan grimaced. "Contesting it would mean war, though. Wouldn't it?"

Sarin finally dropped down into the seat beside Elijah. "We are already at war."

Elijah pondered the possibilities. "What if the Labyrinthine Order were to come forward as supporters of a new claim to the throne? How many mages are there?"

Rue answered before Sarin could. "Enough to give Mirov quite a headache, I imagine. It would take some time to gather them from all corners of the kingdom."

"How much time do we have?" Elijah asked. "Mirov is probably on the move already after everything that happened in the palace dungeon."

"I will send couriers out," Aven said. "I will give them my swiftest horses for their journeys. With any luck, we should have answers -- if not numbers -- by nightfall."

* * *

Nathan managed to escape once the others had dispersed. He'd often fantasized about being a king, about breaking the peasants out of servitude for good, about never having to gather enough money for a loaf of bread.

"You remind me of myself."

Startled, Nathan spun around. He relaxed when he saw Elijah leaning against the wall.

"Sorry. Didn't mean to scare you."

Nathan shrugged. "It's all right. I suppose I'm just nervous."

"I would be, too," Elijah said. "How the hell does anyone process the sudden knowledge that he's royalty?"

"I don't know," Nathan admitted. "But I'll tell you when I find out."

Elijah laughed. "Yeah, you're a lot like I was."

"You speak differently than anyone else I have ever known."

Elijah seemed to mull something over. Then he nodded. "Have you ever heard of a traveler? Someone who doesn't… belong in this world?"

"I've heard tales," Nathan said.

Elijah gestured to himself. "Well, now you can say you've met one."

Nathan studied the man in front of him. Elijah certainly wasn't the kind of evil, mean-spirited person Nathan had heard of in stories of travelers from other worlds. The more Nathan looked, the more he also realized how handsome Elijah was. He felt himself grow flush and he glanced away.

"So…" Elijah cleared his throat. "I'm very rarely wrong about things like this…"

Nathan toyed with the frayed corner of a tapestry hanging on the wall. "What?"

"I don't know if there's a word for it here," Elijah said, "but in my former world, we say someone is gay if he or she is attracted to their same gender."

Nathan froze. He'd never uttered a single word about his desires to anyone. "I…"

"It's okay," Elijah said. "You know Sarin is my lover. You know Rue and Raig are lovers. I'm quite sure there are others out there who are like us, men and women."

Nathan sighed and leaned against the wall. He stared at the stone floor. "Mirov despises people like us. Not quite as much as he hates magic, but enough that it keeps those who feel this way silent."

"So not only is he a magic-hating ass, but he's also a homophobe."

"A what?" Nathan asked, looking up.

"Never mind. My point is, you don't have to hide it anymore."

"I never liked hiding it," Nathan said. "It made me feel ashamed, when a part of me didn't want to feel ashamed."

Elijah approached him and gripped Nathan's shoulders. "Nathan, no one should ever feel ashamed of it. We're perfectly normal. Well, more or less."

Nathan chuckled. "I suppose the ability to wield magic may change the general perception of normal."

"There you two are," Sarin said as he headed into the corridor. "Braden has arrived."

Elijah grinned. "He's safe?"

"Very," Sarin said. "And not alone. He brought fighters with him -- men and women who oppose Mirov at every turn."

"Who is Braden?" Nathan asked.

Elijah smiled. "Incredibly cool bounty hunter. Come on."

Nathan just shook his head and let his two new friends drag him back toward the great hall.

When they walked in, several people stood in front of the dais while Lord Aven and Queen Elsbeth sat on their thrones. Nathan still hadn't been able to call them Mother or Father. He loved his adopted parents, but he found himself growing quite fond of Aven and Elsbeth as well. They were kind and loving, even though they had not seen him since his birth. It felt strange… but good.

The crowd surrounded a man who almost stood

above most of them, at least by a couple of inches. Between the people, Nathan thought he caught a glimpse of long dark brown hair and rugged features.

"It's about time you got here," Elijah announced.

The crowd parted, and the man in the middle grinned. Nathan couldn't look away. Dressed in dark brown pants and a basic white tunic, a bow slung on one shoulder, sword on the opposite hip, the man seemed larger than life. Nathan found himself unable to move a single muscle, not even when Elijah tried to tug him closer for an introduction.

"Elijah! Sarin!" The man hugged Elijah and Sarin. Then his gaze met Nathan's, and his already-seductive voice dropped to a tone reserved for a lover. "And who might this be?"

A shiver chased its way up Nathan's spine. It took him a moment to regain his senses long enough to reply.

"Nathan," he said, extending a hand.

The man's palm connected with his own, skin surprisingly smooth for a bounty hunter. "Braden. It's quite a pleasure."

Elijah coughed, though it sounded suspiciously like a snort.

Nathan nodded. He didn't want to let go of the bounty hunter's hand, and Braden didn't seem to mind. "Likewise."

Braden's smile made Nathan's knees buckle. Only by the grace of the gods did Nathan manage to stay upright.

"Well," Sarin announced. "How about we get you all settled in?"

Only then did Nathan remember they were not alone. After a quick scan of the room, he figured Braden had arrived with nearly thirty people. Several servants entered the great hall, and, soon, the newcomers were led out in different directions.

"Are you hungry?" Elijah asked Braden.

"If it's all the same, I'd like to get washed up before I do anything," Braden replied. "We've been on the road."

Nathan absolutely refused to give free rein to the images in his head of Braden nude, water cascading down muscles.

"Let me show you where your chambers are," Sarin said.

Braden smiled once more at Nathan before following Sarin. Once they were out of earshot, Nathan breathed again.

"He's single," Elijah said.

"Single?"

Elijah nodded. "And a bit lonely, I think."

"What do you know about him?"

"He's a bounty hunter who goes out of his way to make Mirov's life a living hell. Incredibly resourceful, strong…" Elijah grinned. "Sexy."

Nathan wasn't about to deny it. "Yes, but what does he think about younger men?"

"How old are you?"

"Nineteen."

Elijah shrugged. "I have no clue how old Braden is, but, if I had to guess, I'd say he might be about thirty. You won't know until you try, Nathan. It's clear he's attracted to you, too."

"Maybe." Nathan stared at the door Braden had gone through with Sarin. "We'll see."

"In the meantime…" Elijah draped an arm around Nathan's shoulders and steered Nathan toward the dais. "We have a kingdom to build."

Client Has Stopped Responding (Dungeon Crawl 5)

Mychael Black

Elijah has never been the type to fight. Now he has no choice. Mirov's forces march toward them, hell bent on destroying the mages and their supporters. Elijah must stand by his lover Sarin, and with their friends, they must win the battle or face utter destruction.

War is an ugly thing, though, and no one comes out unscathed. For one of them, it is utterly devastating. But hope looms on the horizon, if they can only make it through the night.

Chapter One

Royalty.

Nathan still hadn't quite wrapped his head around the notion that he was royalty, despite what the others had told him. He'd grown up thinking he was nothing more than a peasant, albeit one who hid his magical abilities from everyone. Now, everyone knew. Well, everyone in their little rebellion, anyway. His mother -- his *real* mother -- had magic, too. Queen Elsbeth, though she had yet to claim the title, kept her own magic hidden still. According to Rue, Elijah, Sarin, and everybody else, it seemed, putting Nathan on the throne would be far easier than letting Elsbeth claim it.

"You're quiet this evening."

The one person Nathan had been semi-avoiding now stood behind him. Nathan knew the man's voice, even though they hadn't talked privately since their initial meeting a few weeks ago. Braden was a bounty hunter working for Elsbeth and Aven, Nathan's biological parents. Nathan, however, wanted much more than the man's hunting skills.

"Just... thinking, I guess," Nathan said without turning around.

The air grew warmer. Or maybe it was just the way Nathan's body got too hot whenever Braden neared him. A part of Nathan wanted to lean back and feel the hunter's muscular body against his own, but another part wanted to sink into the stone floor. He'd known for a long time that he preferred men, but he'd never had the chance -- or courage -- to act on such desires.

Braden's soft chuckle twisted Nathan's insides into knots. The hunter's hands rested on Nathan's shoulders, kneading, rubbing, squeezing. "About?"

Nathan shivered. "Wondering how this all happened. How I went from peasant life to…" He gestured helplessly. "This. Royalty status, this place…"

"Anything else?" Braden murmured.

Nathan swallowed, the air thick around them. He felt like he'd stepped into a narrow tunnel, with no room to maneuver except forward or back. "Sort of," he admitted.

A gentle pressure turned him until he faced Braden. The hunter smiled, and Nathan barely had time to process what was happening before it actually happened. Braden's lips touched Nathan's, soft but not at all tentative. Nathan threw caution to the wind. He draped his arms around Braden's neck and opened to the man's kiss. Braden backed him up against the stone wall and gave Nathan exactly what he'd been wanting since they first met.

Every swipe of Braden's tongue across his own sent fire racing through Nathan's body. He'd kissed girls, mainly to appear like the other boys. He'd never kissed another male, though. And he sure as hell didn't remember any kiss leaving him so utterly weak-kneed.

"Well, that answers my next question," Braden murmured on Nathan's kiss-swollen lips.

Nathan blinked up at him. "Which is…?"

Braden smiled. "If this was a mutual attraction."

"Oh, it's definitely mutual." Nathan chuckled. "Just… new. For me, anyway."

"Elijah mentioned something along those lines." Braden took Nathan's hand and stepped back a little. "We don't have to rush into anything, you know."

Nathan sighed. "I honestly don't know what I want to happen, or how to do any of it. I mean, I've been with girls in the past, but…" He grimaced. "I never got the chance to even touch a man, much less do anything more."

"Hey." Braden cupped Nathan's face with one hand, thumb caressing Nathan's bottom lip with a feather-light touch. "Like I said, no rush."

Nathan smiled. "Thanks."

"Come on," Braden said, tugging gently on Nathan's hand. "We're supposed to meet the others in the great hall in half an hour, so we have a little while to get to know each other."

Nathan let the hunter lead him down the corridor and out a side door. A small garden greeted them, surrounded by the stone walls of the keep. Stone benches sat along the sides, and circular ones ringed a stone fountain in the center of the garden. Water trickled down from a howling wolf's mouth, over two pups below, and finally into the large basin at the bottom. Flowering bushes grew in well-tended groups, and small trees pointed upward to the sun shining into the tiny oasis.

Braden followed the pebbled path to one of the benches and sat down, pulling Nathan down beside him. "I haven't been here in some time."

Nathan looked around, bewildered. "I never expected to find someplace like this in the middle of a castle."

"When Aven took control of the keep years ago, the door to the garden had been bricked up," Braden said. "He had several men -- myself included -- knock down the barrier. We had no idea what to expect, but it certainly wasn't a garden. Elsbeth hired caretakers to restore it."

"Where are you from?" Nathan asked. "I know nothing about you."

Braden smiled at him. "I was born in a tiny

village in the northeastern area of the Tasmorum province, but I grew up everywhere. My father was a trader, so we traveled a lot during my childhood. My mother cared for children anywhere we wound up. As a result, I have friends all over Timiria, in every province and most of the cities."

"Wow." Nathan laughed. "Is that why you became a hunter? Because you enjoy moving around a lot?"

Braden shrugged. "For the most part, yes. I love being in the wild, exploring, challenging myself against whatever perils nature throws at me. What about you?"

Nathan sighed. "Well, you know who my real parents are," he said. "My adoptive parents were simple peasants in Cosei. When I turned fourteen, I began working in Mirov's stables to earn money and help my family." He glanced over at Braden, who watched him with a smile. "How old were you when you knew you were... different? That you liked guys and not girls."

"Honestly, I think I've always known," Braden said. "My first experience was with a boy in one of the villages where we lived for a time. He was thirteen, and I was twelve. He gave me my first kiss. I didn't do anything else until I was sixteen and met a man who said he was twenty. I don't know if he was or not, nor did I care. He introduced me to lovemaking between men."

"Did you tell your parents?"

"No. I'd left them to find my own way when I was eighteen. Word reached me that they'd died in a house fire, before I managed to summon the courage to tell them about me."

Nathan grimaced. "I'm sorry."

Braden put his arm around Nathan's shoulders and squeezed. "Thank you. I wasn't overly close to them, but it hurt nonetheless. How about you? When did you find out you liked men?"

"I think I was about fourteen," Nathan said. "I was too scared to do or say anything, though. I didn't know anyone who felt like I did -- not until I met Elijah and Sarin. I've been with girls, but you're the first guy I've ever kissed."

Fingers slipped beneath Nathan's chin and tilted his head until he met Braden's steady, warm brown gaze. When lips touched his own, Nathan closed his eyes and let Braden do anything the man wanted. Nathan turned the slightest bit and draped both arms around the hunter's neck. Braden slid off the bench and eased Nathan onto the soft grass without breaking the kiss.

Nathan opened his legs, cradling Braden between them. The hunter's muscular body felt indescribably amazing where it pressed against Nathan's own lanky form. Braden ran one hand down Nathan's side until it reached Nathan's hip. Trapped in a kiss, Nathan could only wiggle a little, in hopes that the hand would move just a bit more to the middle. Braden chuckled softly.

"I won't do more here. Our first time will be in a proper bed, with something slick to ease the way." Braden finally moved his hand between their bodies, his fingers skimming over the hardening ridge of Nathan's aching cock. "But I can't deny the need to touch you."

"Please," Nathan whispered, hips lifting.

Braden's hand slipped beneath the waistband of Nathan's pants. Warm fingertips brushed the swollen head of Nathan's prick, sending sparks shooting through his body. Nathan moaned and dug his own fingers into Braden's biceps. When the hunter's hand wrapped around the shaft, Nathan bit his tongue to stifle a triumphant shout.

Trapped in the confines of his pants, Nathan squirmed as Braden teased him. The hunter's touches were light, the strokes languid and easy. Nathan wanted to beg the man to speed up, stroke harder, anything.

"Focus on this," Braden whispered on Nathan's lips, giving Nathan's cock a slight squeeze and stroke. "Just think about how good it feels, how amazing it will feel when I'm buried deep inside you, thrusting, rocking…"

Nathan gasped, heart pounding in time to the pulls on his cock. "Don't stop," he panted. His hips jerked upward into every motion, making love to Braden's fist.

"There's a place deep inside you," Braden continued, rubbing the sensitive slit at the tip with his thumb. "When my cock glides over it, pleasure rocks your entire body -- pleasure like nothing you've ever felt before."

Nathan grabbed the man's head and pulled Braden down for a hard kiss. The hunter groaned into Nathan's mouth. The motions on Nathan's cock sped up, stronger, harder. He felt hardness press against his thigh. He pushed up with his leg, and Braden grunted.

"Now," Braden said, breathless. "Come with me."

Braden did something. Nathan had no idea what. But lightning bolts shot up Nathan's spine and through his balls, then out his cock. Semen coated Braden's fist while Nathan cried out the hunter's name. Braden moaned and bucked against Nathan's thigh. Warmth seeped through both layers of cloth.

Panting, they lay on the grass, hearts thundering.

"Wow," Nathan muttered.

Braden chuckled. "And that was just my hand and your leg."

* * *

Elijah sat down beside Sarin. Rue had called everyone to the great hall to discuss the war and their preparations. Elijah honestly didn't know what to do or say. With the exception of Nathan, everyone else had been through war. Elijah rested his head on Sarin's shoulder and listened to Rue, Aven, Raig, and Elsbeth.

"Are you certain you want to abdicate your rightful throne?" Aven asked Elsbeth.

Elsbeth nodded and smiled at Nathan, who sat beside Braden. "I know I'm making the right choice. Nathan has a better chance than a queen whose name has been slandered over the years."

Elijah had to admit: she had a good point. Mirov, the asshole who stole Elsbeth's throne and took it for himself, had raked his magic-wielding sister's name through the mud.

There were pockets of people scattered all over Timiria who still supported her, but, for the most part, Mirov's intense hatred of magic had poisoned the general populace. Everyone knew Elsbeth possessed magic. No one had a clue that Nathan did, though. If Nathan could keep his abilities hidden, maybe he'd actually have a chance.

Nathan sighed. "I have no idea how to be anything other than a peasant. I certainly know nothing of fighting or warfare."

"I can help with both," Aven said. "We would never consider putting you on the throne without any sort of instruction. Ruling as a lord such as myself is difficult enough. Ruling as a king will test every ability you possess."

Chapter Two

Elijah watched as Aven instructed Nathan on how to present himself as a king. Whenever Nathan slouched in the chair, Aven reminded him to sit straight, head held high. Nathan looked like he wanted to bolt the second Aven turned away. Elijah really couldn't blame him, either.

"Is he even ready for this?"

"I honestly don't know," Sarin said. "Aven has been lord of this region for a long time. He's had the practice. Nathan, on the other hand, has spent his entire life as a peasant."

"He will be fine," Braden said as he joined them.

Elijah smirked. "We were discussing his learning how to be a king -- not his experience in bed."

Braden laughed. "In that case, he will be fine with one..." He winked. "And excel in the other."

Sarin rolled his eyes. "And people say I'm bad."

"You are," Elijah answered with a grin. "So..." Elijah nudged Braden with his elbow. "How are you two? Have you talked yet?"

A slow smile spread across Braden's face. "A gentleman doesn't kiss and tell."

Elijah laughed. "Aha! I knew it!"

The doors of the great hall opened, and a scout ran into the hall. "My lord," he said to Aven, out of breath and looking far too alarmed for Elijah's comfort. "We have reports from distant villages of an army amassing outside of Cosei."

Aven cursed under his breath. "Son, we will have to continue your lessons later," he said to Nathan. "Sarin, where is your father?"

"He retired to his chambers with Raig. Shall I

fetch him?"

Aven nodded. "Please. Braden, I need you out there." The lord approached Braden, voice lowering. "I must know what Mirov is planning. Be swift."

Something flashed in Braden's eyes for the briefest moment. Then it was gone. "Yes, my lord."

Elijah watched the hunter walk out of the great hall. Aven went to speak with the scout, and Elijah headed over to Nathan. The young man seemed far less confident with the news of an army.

"How am I going to do this?"

Elijah sighed and sat on the dais steps just below the throne where Nathan sat. "If I had the answer to that, you'd be the first to hear it. So how are you and Braden?"

Nathan grinned. "Good. We... kissed," he said, though the blush that colored his cheeks told Elijah they'd done far more than kiss. "Can I ask you something?"

"Sure."

Nathan glanced up at the massive doors of the great hall. "You met Braden before me. Did you ever notice anything weird about him?"

"Well, beyond his nonchalance when killing bandits and rogue mages, not really. I mean, he's fast." Elijah thought about the bandit camp they'd raided in order to get a head for a glamor spell. "Okay, *really* fast." He looked at Nathan. "Why?"

Nathan shrugged. "Just a gut feeling, I guess. I really, really like him. But there's something different about Braden. Not bad, just... different."

Sarin rejoined them, while Rue and Raig went to speak with Aven. "Where is Braden?"

"Scouting," Elijah answered. "Hey, got a question for you. Have you noticed anything strange about Braden?"

Sarin glanced at Aven, then crouched, his voice lowering only for Elijah and Nathan. "No one knows this beyond Elsbeth and Aven. I found out because I overheard them talking to him. Braden is an oscen."

Nathan blinked. "He's a shapeshifter?"

Elijah vaguely recalled the oscen race as being one of the races available during the game's character creation process. The oscens were avian shapeshifters. Most of their animal forms were ravens, owls, or crows. Elijah wondered which form Braden could take.

Sarin nodded. "He can become a raven at will."

"Wow." Despite how many games he'd played over the years, Elijah had a hard time picturing a grown man -- especially one as tall and muscular as Braden -- turning into something as small as a bird. "The biology alone is screwing with my head."

"It's nature magic," Sarin said. "In the same way I can change into a wolf, though oscens are born with it. They aren't granted the ability by any deity."

"So… Braden is a mage?" Elijah asked.

Sarin nodded. "He is, though, for obvious reasons, no one knows. Oscens can blend into human society with ease."

* * *

The world passed by below, the woods curiously quiet. Braden had been flying for the entire day, but this was the first time he'd noticed something… off. He dipped lower and coasted through the trees. The lack of movement, of sound, made him uneasy. He knew Timiria's forests better than most. Only the ones farthest south, in the colder climates, were ever this devoid of activity. It seemed as if the denizens hid from a danger no one else could see.

Just as he readied to ascend once more, he spotted the flicker of a distant fire. As he approached it, he realized there were more than one. Beyond the four campfires clustered together, many more spread out, stretching outside of the forest and into fields.

Braden landed on a tree branch and preened his wing feathers when a soldier glanced in his direction. Ravens were not uncommon, but they tended to be nocturnal. The soldier set down a metal cup and picked up a bow. Braden's feathers bristled, and he lifted off. He didn't make it through the top of the tree branches before the arrow grazed his left wing. The arrow didn't pierce it, but the skin tore. Pain lanced through him. That had been no regular arrow. He had to get out.

Leaves rustled from behind him, and several men neared. He wasn't moving as fast as he should have been. Blood seeped from his torn wing. Whatever poison the arrow had been laced with seared through Braden's blood. His wing felt as if it were on fire. Shouts filled the forest. He managed to find a tree just far enough away to prevent anyone seeing him.

Soldiers ran past the tree, oblivious to his hiding place. He remained silent as the grave. Somehow, some way, the soldier who'd shot at him had known what Braden was. That knowledge landed like a lead weight in Braden's gut. How could a regular human have any clue? Oscens were normally able to blend in with no one the wiser.

"Where is it?" The soldier who'd fire the arrow looked around, far too close to the tree for Braden's comfort. "Damned shapeshifter spy!"

One of the others joined the soldier. "Captain, we can find no evidence of him."

The captain snarled. "Back to camp then!" he

ordered his men. "Those mages will get a nasty surprise."

After several minutes, the men returned to their fires and meals. Braden waited another few minutes, scanning the woods below, before carefully leaving his hole. He flew as swiftly as possible.

The sun had begun to set by the time Braden reached the fortified walls of Pelarum. Instead of shifting before entering the town, he flew right over the wall and landed on the keep's front steps. He shifted and pushed open the doors, only to collapse just inside the great hall.

"Braden!"

The world turned fuzzy, and sounds were muffled. Braden had enough senses left to realize his head didn't hit the cold stone floor, though.

* * *

"Poison."

Everyone looked up at Rue as if he could cure Braden. He honestly had no idea if he could. He sighed and dropped onto a chair. His lover's big hands began working the tension out of Rue's shoulders.

"Do you know what kind?" Nathan asked him. "Is there anything you can do?"

Elsbeth glanced around the table at them all before speaking. "At this point, I don't think it is an issue of divulging such a secret. Braden -- and we -- trust you all with the knowledge. He is an oscen, and he has been in our service since he turned eighteen."

Rue nodded, noticing that Nathan, Sarin, and Elijah didn't seem too surprised. Rue knew Nathan and Braden were drawn to one another, but he didn't have the heart to lie. "I don't know if I can cure it. From my research on the symptoms, this poison affects only oscens. Braden's fever has spiked. This was no accident. *Someone* knew how to cripple an oscen. His left arm has stopped bleeding, at least."

"Do we know what happened?" Aven asked.

Rue shook his head. "Braden's mutterings are primarily fever-fueled ramblings, but I managed to discern enough to learn that Mirov's men knew what Braden is. My question is, how did the soldiers know?"

Sarin stood and started pacing, a sure sign he was thinking, mulling over things. He'd done it since he was a child. "Mirov is driven by his hatred of magic. Elsbeth is known to possess it. Mirov has poisoned the people against her because she is a mage. What are the chances that he actually has magic-users, even oscens, in his employ?"

"He'd never allow it," Elsbeth said. "He would have executed them without giving it a second thought."

"But what if he doesn't *know*," Sarin argued.

"Why on earth would any mages or oscens work for someone like Mirov?" Elijah asked.

It didn't make much sense to Rue either. "That's a very good question, but another oscen would know what Braden is. Their auras have a signature that only others of their kind can see. Which means at least one of the soldiers who attacked Braden -- maybe even the one who shot him -- knew what he is. There are only a handful of poisons that can disable an oscen. That much I do know."

"How is he, otherwise?" Aven asked. "I don't mean to sound callous -- Braden is a dear friend -- but we need to know what he found."

"I... am well enough."

Everyone turned to see Braden leaning against the doorframe leading into the living quarters wing of the keep. Nathan jumped up and rushed to Braden. Braden smiled and bent down for a kiss. Then Nathan led him toward the table where the others waited. Braden winced a bit as he sat down.

"I would have come to you," Aven said.

Braden smirked. "If I recall, you're the one who's told me on numerous occasions that I'm terminally stubborn." His expression turned serious, despite the pain. "The one who shot me was not an oscen, but a mage can mimic the ability using spells. There were four fires at the head, but the bulk of Mirov's army is there. Far too many fires to count."

"Do you think any of your kind would willingly join him?" Rue asked.

Braden shrugged. "Oscens are as varied in temperament and personality as humans. Technically, we are nature mages, but that doesn't mean some outright disagree with Mirov and his convictions. Just don't ask me why."

Rue didn't have a reasonable answer either. "How long do you think we have?"

"One day, maybe two," Braden said. "It only took me a day to reach their encampment, but I didn't have an entire army to coordinate on the move. Either way, we need to prepare as if they will arrive in the morning." He seemed to slump a little. Nathan stood and whispered something in Braden's ear. After a moment, Braden nodded and got up. "If you will excuse us," he said, looking pale again. "I fear I may have gotten out of bed rather prematurely."

Nathan led Braden out of the great hall. Sarin sat back down, expressions of confusion, determination, and anger all rolled into one telltale grimace. Rue didn't blame his son. None of this made any sense whatsoever.

"So what is the plan?" Elijah asked, eyeing each of them in turn. "I'm willing to bet Mirov has far more soldiers than we do."

Aven glanced at Rue. "Is there any possible way to summon the rest of your order in time?"

"There is, but it takes half a day to prepare the spell and another half-day to recover from it. However, I believe that if I have help, I can expedite things." Rue knew Sarin would do it willingly, but he wasn't sure about Nathan or Elsbeth.

"You have my magic," Elsbeth announced. "And, though I speak for him, I think Nathan would gladly say the same. What do you need from us?"

* * *

Elijah shouldered his quiver and picked up his bow. He would have preferred to have Sarin come with him, but Sarin -- like Elsbeth, Rue, and Nathan -- had to prepare for the spell the four of them would cast to contact the rest of the Labyrinthine Order of mages.

"Move as silently as possible," Rue said from where he sat on the bed. "The ingredients you're looking for are here." He held out a tied scroll. "Four herbs, two types of mushrooms, and the abdomen of a lightbug."

Elijah bit his tongue. The list sounded like every other item-gathering quest he'd done in countless games. He slipped the scroll beneath his belt. "Got it. Hopefully this won't take long."

Sarin entered a moment later. After Rue excused himself from the room, Sarin pulled Elijah close. "Please, please be careful. I can't lose you."

Elijah smiled and kissed his beloved mage. "You won't. I promise."

Nodding, Sarin let go and stepped back. "I -- we

-- eagerly await your return. I love you."

"Love you, too."

Elijah headed out. Guards shut the outer wall's gates behind him, leaving him alone to face the expanse of wilderness beyond the fortress. He unrolled the scroll and looked through the list. Thankfully, Rue had drawn rudimentary pictures of the herbs and mushrooms for him, along with notes on where Elijah could find them. In the distance, a tiny yellow light blinked. Then another flickered a bit further away. Replacing the scroll beneath his belt, Elijah headed toward the general area.

Several fireflies flitted around, and he managed to catch one between his palms. Only then did he realize he had nothing to put the bug in while he continued his search. Sighing, he released the bug.

"Okay, so I'll be back after I get the rest."

He opened up the scroll again and studied the pictures. The first herb -- elecus root -- could be found at the base of water-bound trees. The root looked like a demon claw, but dark orange in color.

Elijah went to the edge of the nearest stream and spotted a tree that nearly sat in the water. He crouched and found the elecus root growing right at the water's edge. He picked the root carefully and tucked it into a small pouch Rue had given him.

After consulting the scroll again, he went in search of selenon -- a mossy-looking herb that grew in patches around boulders. He found a small section and tucked some into the pouch.

"Next," he muttered as he read the list. "Deathskunk." That didn't sound pleasant.

He continued into the nearest woods and froze.

"Oh, fuck, that's foul!" He covered his nose and peered down at the zombie-green, tangled plant at his feet. No fucking wonder it was called deathskunk. He tried not to retch as he shoved a handful into the pouch.

To his right, he saw a clump of bright red flowers. Judging by the picture on the scroll, the flowers were the last herb: argon. He plucked several flowers and put them into the pouch with the rest.

By the time he found the two mushrooms, it was getting dark. He headed back toward the keep, catching a firefly on the way. When he got to the gates, the guards opened it for him.

Rue waited near what looked like a chapel. "Wonderful," he said as he took the pouch from Elijah.

"Not sure what to do about this." Elijah opened his hand just enough for Rue to see the bug.

Rue took it from him and, without hesitation, pulled the firefly apart. The mage shrugged. "One firefly or countless lives? I think it would understand." Ingredients in hand, Rue went into the chapel. Elijah followed. "You can witness the spell but do not speak. We need no interruptions."

Nodding, Elijah sat on a bench near the door. Rue, Sarin, Nathan, and Elsbeth all stood at the front where an altar normally would be. Rue lit something inside an iron cauldron in the middle, and flames flared upward several feet. Rue began chanting quietly, though Elijah couldn't hear the words.

A few seconds later, Sarin joined in. Then Nathan, and then Elsbeth.

The round-robin chanting grew louder, but Elijah still had no idea what they said. The flames swirled upward, and smoke curled around each of them. When Rue stopped chanting, the others continued.

"Brothers and sisters, we have need of you. Pelarum -- and all our kind -- will soon be under attack. Mirov seeks to destroy all magic in this world. We beseech you: join us before the morrow."

The chanting stopped abruptly. The smoke and fire both seemed to get sucked back into the cauldron.

"It is done," Rue said. "Now we must all prepare for war."

Chapter Three

Nathan collapsed onto the bed beside Braden. "That took more out of me -- all of us -- than I expected."

Braden rolled onto one side to face Nathan. The man's arm had healed significantly over the past few hours, and his fever had finally broken. "Are you all right?"

Nathan nodded. "Yes. I've never done anything like that, though. I grew up hiding my magic, and now I'm able to use it somewhat freely. It's weird, but it feels kind of good to not hide it."

Braden smiled and leaned down to kiss Nathan softly. "I can understand that. Oscens don't openly display their shapeshifting abilities for the same reasons. Natural or not, it's still considered magic."

Nathan studied the man's face, taking in the handsome ruggedness that had caught his eye when they first met. "Are you scared?"

"War is always terrifying," Braden said. "No matter how many battles you go through, no matter how many lives you take, don't ever become numb to it. When you become numb to death, you're no less a monster than Mirov. Every soul is worthy of respect, even in death."

"Even Mirov?"

Braden nodded. "Even Mirov. When he dies, whether in battle or after a fair trial, he will be buried, as is custom for his people."

Nathan wanted to argue, but he didn't. He sighed. "Rue said we have to rest before we do anything else. The spell saps a lot out of us." He smiled slowly, gaze sliding down Braden's body. "But..."

Braden surprised him by rolling over and kneeling between his legs. The hunter's body felt amazing where it pressed all along Nathan's, their cocks both hard and pushing against each other through their clothes. Nathan ran his hands up Braden's sides, fingers mapping the muscles of his lover's back. Nathan had never wanted anyone like he wanted Braden. He craved the hunter's touch, kiss, everything.

"Are you ready for this?" Braden murmured in Nathan's ear. He kept himself propped on his right arm, while his recently-healed left one coasted down Nathan's side to grip Nathan's hip. "I will never hurt you."

Nathan groaned and dug his fingers into Braden's bare skin. He swore he felt where the man's wings appeared when in bird form. "I need you. I've never needed anyone this much." In all honesty, it scared the hell out of him, how strongly he felt for Braden.

Braden slipped his hand between them to untie Nathan's pants. Nathan lifted his hips, and Braden worked the pants down and off. Bared to his hunter's gaze, Nathan couldn't stop the way his cock thickened and stood at attention. His breath whooshed out of his lungs the second Braden's long fingers wrapped around his shaft.

"Gods, that..." Nathan moaned as Braden's fist began working him up and down. "Please..."

Braden kissed a path along Nathan's jaw, down his neck. "Do you value this shirt?"

Nathan shook his head. Braden released him and, gripping the neckline of the shirt, tore the cloth and tossed the remnants on the floor. Nathan gasped, the incident shocking but hot as hell. Then Braden slid down his body.

"Has anyone ever taken you into their mouth?"

"Once, a girl."

Braden grinned and circled the base of Nathan's hard cock with his thumb and fingers. Then the hunter's lips descended over the tip, sucking the head into the intense heat of Braden's mouth.

"Oh, gods. Braden. Yes!"

Nathan grabbed the hunter's head and thrust into Braden's mouth, unable to hold back. The sucking, the licking, the stroking… it didn't take long. Nathan shouted Braden's name as he shot his release down the man's throat.

Braden licked him clean, then moved back up. "That was hot."

Nathan would have agreed, would have said something, but words refused to come out. He'd had it done by a girl, but knowing a man had done that just made the whole experience unbelievably intense.

Braden gently nudged Nathan's legs open more, and something cool and slick touched Nathan's hole. Nathan tensed for a moment, but Braden kissed him. Two fingers circled the puckered entrance, not quite pushing inside. Braden's tongue scrambled Nathan's brain as it swept through his mouth. The hunter fed him low, sexy groans, as a hard cock rested between Nathan's legs. The head barely brushed his skin, but it was enough to make Nathan ache for more.

Nathan swallowed the trepidation and rocked his hips downward. Braden's fingers entered him, gliding slick and slow until the hunter's knuckles touched Nathan's body. They both stilled, breathing hard, heavy.

"Gods, you're tight," Braden murmured. "So hot, it makes me crazy with need."

The fingers inside him scissored, and Nathan moaned. "Yes... more..."

A third finger joined the first two. The burn felt exquisite. He'd never even touched himself there, though he'd been tempted in the past. He never expected it to feel so... amazingly wonderful.

"Braden. Please. I need you."

Braden eased his fingers out and slicked up his cock. "Relax." He rubbed the head over Nathan's hole and pushed in a tiny bit. "Focus on me," he whispered. "Look in my eyes."

When Nathan did, it took his breath away. Braden's eyes were wild, full of adoration and lust. Braden mouthed, "Deep breath."

Nathan inhaled, gaze locked onto Braden's. Pressure and fullness overwhelmed him. He gripped Braden's biceps, and his toes curled. The hunter stopped just as the head entered Nathan's body.

"It's..." Nathan shook his head, unable to find the words.

"I know."

Braden kissed him. While Nathan's mind stayed on the man's lips, Braden's cock sank deep into Nathan's body. The world sort of spun in dizzying circles. Nathan began to shake, his heart thundering and threatening to burst through his ribcage. Braden started moving, slow and easy, in and out. Kisses covered Nathan's lips, jaw, neck. Braden's breath warmed Nathan's skin.

Sensations swept through Nathan, unlike anything he'd ever felt before. The fullness made him weak in the knees and drove him mad. He never wanted this to end. Legs locking around Braden's waist, Nathan arched as sparks shot up his spine. Every thrust, every touch deep inside him all spurred him toward the edge.

"Now," Braden gasped. He did something, moved his hips in a way that sent lightning shooting up Nathan's spine.

Nathan bucked, crying out when it all slammed into him at once. Semen spurted onto their torsos, and his hole clamped tight around Braden. Braden let out a low, feral groan, and then thick heat pulsed into Nathan's body with every jerk of Braden's hips.

It took several moments before either of them could do so much as move. Braden withdrew, slowly, and found his own shirt to wipe them both clean. Then he rolled onto his back and gathered Nathan to him.

"That was…" Braden shook his head. "There are no words to describe how it felt."

Nodding, Nathan curled up into his hunter's side, head on Braden's shoulder. Despite the looming war, Braden's heartbeat lulled him to sleep.

* * *

Elijah woke to shouts from outside the keep. When he rolled over, he discovered himself alone. Horse hooves thundered through the small courtyard, then abruptly stopped. Elijah got up and peered out the window. He spotted Sarin and Rue talking with several men and women he hadn't seen before.

Another, much larger group handed off their horses' reins to stable boys and joined the others. Although he couldn't see any distinguishing marks, Elijah figured these were the rest of Rue and Sarin's order. Most of the mages were younger, somewhere between Nathan and Sarin's ages, though a few seemed to be at least as old as Rue.

Elijah got dressed and headed downstairs. Servants hurried to set out what looked like a breakfast banquet in the main hall, and the door to Aven's private study stood ajar. Before he got past the door, Aven called for him. Elijah backed up and peered into the room.

"Please, come in," Aven said, gesturing to one of the cushioned chairs.

Several men and women sat on the remaining chairs and couches. Every single one of them wore armor made of chain and plate. Elijah took the offered seat beside Aven.

"Elijah, allow me to introduce my commanders. They will take the lead when the time comes to meet Mirov on the battlefield. My friends, this is Elijah, lover and Sentinel of Sarin Eckhert. He will be marching with us, though his place -- like all Sentinels -- is with his mage."

Elijah nodded. "Pleased to meet you all." He looked to Aven. "I have never been in any kind of battle, you know."

"Neither have most of our mages," Aven replied. He sighed. "Most of them are younger than Sarin, though older than my son. None of them has ever needed to train for war. Small skirmishes here and there, yes. But this is far different."

One of the commanders, an older woman who looked like she could have been Sarin's mother, spoke up. "I have heard much about you, Master Elijah. I am Gwen, sister to Rue, aunt to your mage."

"No wonder you look like Sarin."

She chuckled. "It is not common knowledge, for obvious reasons. We have kept our relation secret but to a few. You say you have not fought. I also would wager a guess that you are not from here."

"You'd be right. I'm... a traveler," Elijah said. He glanced at each commander, but no one did so much as raise an eyebrow. "But, even in my own world, I learned archery. Sarin has taught me a few things with a sword, but I prefer standing out of range of anything sharp."

Gwen nodded. "You will find that such skills are highly prized. Not all commanders rely on the sword. I much prefer the bow myself."

That made Elijah feel a bit better. He'd been wondering just how well he'd fit in -- much less be openly accepted -- if people knew his lack of battle prowess. Knowing he'd be with the mages helped, too.

"Are there other Sentinels? I'm assuming yes, since we have the rest of Sarin's order here."

"We do," Aven said. "Elsbeth will be using her own magic, and I am her Sentinel. Nathan has decided to keep his magic hidden, but Braden will remain at his side. Of course, there is also Rue, with Raig as his Sentinel. Don't worry. Every mage has a Sentinel. As one yourself, you need to be aware of your duties."

Another commander, one who looked to be about Sarin's age, spoke. "A Sentinel must place him or herself between their mage and any danger. Your mage has to keep focused, and it is your job to make sure that concentration is not broken by some brute with a sword or axe. Always stay sharp, wary of anything that could harm or hinder your mage. When a mage casts a spell, it leaves him or her open and vulnerable. That is the best time for an attacker to strike. Never lower your guard, especially at that moment."

"You're a Sentinel, aren't you?"

The commander smiled. "I am. My name is Elric, and my mage is Elandra. She is with the others now, but I will be at her side, ready to die in order to protect her."

Elijah had the feeling there was far more to being

a Sentinel than just… protecting. "So, here's a question, somewhat unrelated to battle. Are all Sentinels and their mages romantically involved?"

"Not at all," the commander said. "Elandra is my twin sister, and the mother of my nieces."

Okay, that made sense.

"You know what your duties are," Aven said. "Do you have any questions?"

Elijah sighed. "Just one. How the hell are we going to beat an entire army?"

Chapter Four

"Elijah!"

Elijah joined his lover, letting Sarin draw him into the small group. Many of the men and women Elijah had seen earlier now sat around several tables, chatting and eating. Armored companions sat beside each one, and Elijah recognized the twins, the mage Elandra and Elric, her brother-turned-Sentinel.

"Love, I want you to meet some friends." Sarin waited until Elijah sat down. "This is Elandra and her brother, and Sentinel, Elric." Elric held up his cup in greeting. Elandra waved. "Here, we have a husband-and-wife team, the mage Jon and his Sentinel-wife, Cass. Finally, there are sisters Chanie and Carly."

"Good to meet you all," Elijah said. "I've heard a lot about the order, especially in the past couple of days."

"Someone told me you're a traveler," Chanie said. "What is your home like?"

Elijah glanced at each of them in turn, at Sarin, and finally back to Chanie. "This is home. Though I came from… elsewhere, I would never leave this place. Nor would I ever leave Sarin."

They all cheered and lifted their cups in salute and agreement. Elijah leaned on Sarin's shoulder and felt the mage kiss the top of his head. He'd thought about what it would be like to return to his version of Earth, but the more he mulled it over, the more he realized he'd never do it. He'd been forced into a closet, lived in absolute misery and loneliness. Here, he was valued and had friends he knew, without a doubt, he could count on. Then there was Sarin.

The one thing Elijah never expected to have, he

now refused to even consider walking away from. He lifted his head for a kiss, which Sarin gave freely. No one uttered a single nasty comment. No one got up and left the table due to the open display of affection. Hell, when Elijah looked, he noticed Rue and Raig doing much the same thing with no repercussions. And Rue was the Elder of the entire order.

"Well," Elandra said, "I think I speak for all of us when I say that I hope you stay here with us. I've known Sarin nearly all my life, and I have never seen him so happy."

Elijah smiled. "I've never been this happy. Believe me, I'm not going anywhere, unless it's at Sarin's side."

Aven stood at the middle of the long table that stretched across the dais. "My friends, may I have your attention?" Everyone quieted and focused on him. "Tomorrow, we will meet Mirov in battle. We will fight for those we love." He smiled at Elsbeth. "But we also fight for all the people of this land. When Mirov is defeated, our son -- Nathan -- will take the throne in Elsbeth's stead. So this toast is to your future king!"

Everyone raised their cups and cheered, while Nathan turned bright red and tried to hide in Braden's lap. Elijah laughed and toasted his friend. Despite the worry and shyness, he had a feeling Nathan would do just fine as a king. Aven and Elsbeth wouldn't let their son flounder without some kind of direction and help. The announcement of his lineage had apparently been given beforehand, since no one seemed too surprised. It was also no secret that Nathan was a mage.

"I thought Nathan's magic would be kept hidden," Elijah whispered to Sarin when everyone resumed their own loud conversations.

"In this group, he is safe -- both in magic and

lineage. Outside of it, to the general populace, he is simply a young man who will, eventually, become their king."

"He looks scared to death."

Sarin nodded. "Anyone would be, I imagine. I highly doubt this is the life he expected to lead when he became a man."

"At what age do kids officially reach adulthood, anyway?"

"Sixteen," Sarin said. "Some are married, whether by arrangement or not. Some remain unmarried but with lovers. It is not an issue, even for the women. Either gender may initiate sex or marriage, without societal condemnation. Magic is the only stigma in our world."

"They wouldn't think that way if they had a mage like you," Elijah muttered.

Sarin leaned close and whispered, "But I am all yours, my love. Every inch of me."

Elijah shivered. "That you are."

* * *

Elijah's back hit the door, but he didn't give a damn. He groaned as Sarin bit and nipped a path along his jaw and down his neck. The mage's breath warmed Elijah's skin, and the man's hands made quick work of Elijah's clothes. Elijah did his best to help, but Sarin moved away.

"Bed," the mage said as he stripped off his shirt.

The sight of the broad chest, covered in the magic, furred swirls of Sarin's magic, made Elijah's knees weak. Elijah tossed his clothing to the side and sprawled out on the bed. Sarin, still wearing pants, knelt between Elijah's thighs.

"You're not naked," Elijah muttered. The words

morphed into a moan when Sarin's lips closed around the head of Elijah's cock. "Oh, fuck," he gasped. Elijah gripped the blanket beneath him, fisting it when Sarin sucked him down. "Oh, my God. Sarin."

The mage moaned, and the vibration felt like a shockwave. Elijah bucked, thrusting deeper into Sarin's mouth. Two slick fingers pushed inside him with no warning, and Elijah rocked his hips down to drive them deeper. Sarin set up a fast, dizzying rhythm of sucking and fingering, driving Elijah out of his fucking mind.

"Now!" Elijah shouted as he struggled to hold back an orgasm.

Sarin refused. A third finger plunged into Elijah, setting off a chain reaction. Elijah bucked and thrust, shooting his load down his lover's throat. Only then did Sarin back off and withdraw his fingers. He licked Elijah's cock clean and grinned.

"My turn."

Without giving Elijah a chance to say a word, Sarin flipped Elijah over. Elijah groaned when the mage spread his cheeks apart. Sarin's tongue flicked over Elijah's hole, then pressed inside. Elijah wanted to rock backward, but Sarin held onto his hips, keeping him still. Every swipe of that tongue threatened to renew Elijah's cock.

Sarin stopped and leaned over Elijah's back. The mage had, at some point, managed to get rid of the pants. Bare skin covered Elijah's, and a hard, thick cock pressed at his waiting ass. "Ready?"

"Always."

Like any good mage, Sarin conjured up something slick, though, if Elijah had to guess, the man grabbed the jar out of the bedside table. Then the blunt, thick head of Sarin's cock began pushing into Elijah's body. Elijah made himself relax, despite wanting Sarin to just pound him into the bed. By the time the mage had buried his full length, Elijah was shaking.

"For God's sake, just fuck me," Elijah muttered.

Sarin chuckled. He braced himself up off of Elijah and began moving in and out, the strokes slow and easy. Elijah grumbled and drew his legs up a bit, angling his ass down. Quick to take a hint, Sarin grabbed Elijah's hips and gave Elijah exactly what he'd asked for.

The headboard thudded against the wall, and the wooden bed creaked. Elijah shoved a hand under himself and gripped his cock. He pumped it in time to Sarin's hard, deep thrusts, gasping and panting into the blanket.

The cock buried inside him began swelling, stretching Elijah's ass even more. Elijah whimpered, and his strokes stuttered a bit. When Sarin did *that* magic, nothing else in the world fucking existed. The mage grunted and, with one final, hard thrust, came. Elijah followed right behind him, the throb of the man's cock the best trigger ever.

Breathless, Elijah collapsed onto the bed, grimacing at the wet spot but not caring enough to move. He hissed softly as Sarin eased out of him. Something soft and warm wiped the lube and spunk off. Then Sarin snuggled up beside him.

"If anyone ever accuses me of being a size queen, I'm blaming you."

Sarin snickered. "And I'd wholeheartedly take the blame."

Elijah grumbled. "Shirt?"

Sarin reached down for one of their shirts and handed it over. Elijah rolled to wipe his belly and the bed, then spread the shirt enough to keep him off the mess. He rested once more beside Sarin, head on his mage's shoulder. They remained silent for a while, their breathing almost in sync. It started to lull Elijah to sleep, but the impending battle kept him awake.

"Are you scared?"

"Yes," Sarin replied. "Anyone who says otherwise is a liar."

"Have you ever been in any actual battles?"

"Unfortunately, yes. One, but it was one too many. I dislike war. Hell, most of my kind do. Our goddess does not condone such things until there are no other options remaining. She is a peaceful, loving goddess. Not a warmonger. No. Mirov, whatever gods he worships, is the one who gleefully jumps into the fray, sword swinging, with no care for the consequences."

Elijah played with a strand of Sarin's black hair, twirling it around his finger. "Can we beat him? Mirov has an entire army."

"It won't be painless. We will likely suffer casualties. But so will he. War is never victimless. He may have an army, but we have magic and the passion of our Sentinels."

Elijah nodded. It made perfect sense when put like that. There wasn't anything he wouldn't do for Sarin, and he figured the same held true for the other Sentinels. They'd all been chosen, in whatever way, because of their dedication to their respective mages. Granted, Elijah had been chosen before he even knew this world existed, when the thief Elian Sturgis ran amok. Now, though, that life belonged to Elijah.

"You seem rather lost in thought."

Elijah shrugged. "Just remembering how I got here. Wondering how things would have turned out if I hadn't shown up at all. I mean, would Elian be here, right now, ready to march into war with you?"

Sarin shifted until they faced one another. "He would. Sometimes, it's hard for me to recall details about life before you came. There are... differences. Subtle, but there. But the biggest thing you have in common is right here." He placed his hand on Elijah's chest, over Elijah's heart. "When it comes to doing what needs to be done, you do the exact same thing I would expect of Elian."

"Do you miss him?"

Sarin smiled. Not wistful or longing. Just... a smile. "I can't miss him. You *are* Elian. Your personality, your convictions, even the way you kiss. It's all the same. I don't mourn the loss of Elian because I haven't lost him. If anything, you -- Elijah -- have only given me more to love."

Elijah pushed Sarin onto his back and straddled him. "Love you, too. God, how could anyone not love you?"

A knock sounded at the door, and Elijah grumbled. He got up and grabbed his pants. After making sure everything was tucked in where it should be, he opened the door.

"I apologize for the interruption," Braden said, glancing over Elijah's shoulder. "Aven has called everyone to the great hall."

"What's wrong?" Sarin asked.

"Scouts report that Mirov is on the move, using the cover of night in hopes of making a surprise attack before dawn."

"Shit!" Elijah rushed to get dressed while Sarin did the same. "We're on our way."

Braden nodded and left. As soon as they were dressed, Sarin and Elijah headed out. They entered the great hall, only to find that every mage, Sentinel, commander, and soldier filled the room to capacity. There were far more than Elijah had ever thought could fit into the small keep. Instead of sitting on his throne, Aven walked the length of the room, flanked by his army. Elsbeth stayed at the end near the dais, but she wore armor.

"The latest reports put Mirov at half a day's ride," one of the soldiers -- a scout, Elijah assumed -- said.

"Then the bastard drove his men all damn night." Aven seemed to mull something over. "We can use this to our advantage. His men have likely had little rest. If we let them press their advance, we can hold off a siege while our mages pick away at his army from the protection of the walls."

"Will that work?" Elijah whispered to Sarin.

Sarin nodded slightly. "It could. It would lessen our losses, definitely."

"I want the soldiers at the gates and in the courtyard. Archers, use the towers. Sentinels and mages, stay to the walls. With his men weakened, Mirov has very little chance. Ready yourselves. The moment our scouts report sign of Mirov's army, I want everyone in position. Dismissed."

Everyone left, though Aven gestured for Elijah and Sarin to wait. Elsbeth, Nathan, Braden, Rue, and Raig joined them. Servants brought chain and plate armor to the Sentinels, and chain for the mages. Elijah helped Sarin get suited before his mage returned the favor. The armor weighed a ton. Elijah swore he sank into the stone floor.

"This is it," Aven said. "Whatever happens from here, know that I love each and every one of you. Should I fall, I ask only that you protect Elsbeth and Nathan. The throne belongs to our son. Let no one take that from him."

They all said their goodbyes, and then they left to find the best positions.

Rue and Raig made it to the wall first. Raig kissed Rue before taking his place at the mage's side. Elsbeth and Aven stood beside them. Braden and Nathan went up into one of the towers. Despite being a mage, with Braden as his Sentinel, Nathan wouldn't be using his magic. He checked his bow while Braden did the same.

Elijah stepped up to the crenellated wall and peered down at the forest just beyond it. Somewhere, out there, Mirov's army marched toward them. Sarin went over to Rue, and the two of them embraced for several moments. Rue whispered something, and Sarin nodded. Then Rue kissed his son's head.

"You okay?" Elijah asked when Sarin returned to him.

"Yes. Just…" Sarin sighed. "He's the oldest of our kind. Not to say he isn't skilled. Far from it, actually. I just worry."

Bow in one hand, Elijah cupped the back of Sarin's head with the other. "I love you. We can make it through this. All of us."

Sarin smiled. "I pray you're right, love."

Chapter Five

The air felt... electric. Like energy sizzled around them all. It crawled over Elijah's skin, and his hands alternated between sweaty and twitchy. Aven spoke to several important-looking men, commanders possibly. Everyone -- mage, Sentinel, regular soldier -- seemed on edge, as if waiting for the end of the world. Elijah hated the sensation. If they survived this, he never wanted to see another battle in his lifetime.

A scout, scope in hand, raced down the ramps of one of the towers. He said something to Aven, and Aven nodded. No words spoken, Aven gestured for everyone to ready themselves. Elijah realized one of their key advantages was the element of surprise. Mirov had no idea they knew he was coming.

"So it begins," Sarin said.

Though he saw no lights, Elijah heard the rustle of leaves and branches as Mirov's men moved through the trees of the nearby forest. He gripped his bow tighter, forcing himself to remain as still as humanly possible.

Twigs snapped, and armed men rushed from the cover of the trees, shouting, swords and axes held high. Wave after wave spilled out of the forest.

"Archers!" Aven shouted, startling the attackers for the briefest moment. "Fire!"

Arrows from Aven's archers rained down onto the army, bringing down one soldier after another. A pack of men bearing a giant log with one sharpened end headed for the gate, flanked by swordsmen to protect them. The wooden gate shook and rattled from the soldiers banging into it with the battering ram.

"Mages!" Elsbeth conjured a ball of blue fire.

"Now!"

Fireballs of various colors lit up the night and hurled onto the battlefield. Soldiers from Mirov's army shrieked and screamed as they caught fire. Elijah shot arrow after arrow, taking down as many as he could. The sounds of the dying and the war cries of the living filled the air, frightening and deafening.

"Ladders!" someone yelled.

Wood clattered against the wall. Elijah grabbed his knife and stabbed a hand that appeared on the ledge. The soldier screamed and fell backward, the ladder going with him. Elijah and the other archers launched another volley in hopes of taking down the rest of the laddermen before they reached the walls. Mages set fire and sent bolts of lightning down onto the men who scrambled at the tops of the ladders.

An armor-clad brute rode out of the forest on a gigantic horse. "Kill them!"

* * *

A few soldiers managed to breach the top of the wall. Aven's swordsmen pressed them backward, swords clanging against mail and metal. Raig shoved Rue behind him when a soldier rushed forward. Rue barely had time to duck when another sword swung at him.

"Raig!"

The sword collided with Raig's, both attackers hitting from two directions. Rue summoned lightning. It bolted down onto the right attacker. The soldier jerked wildly, and smoke billowed from his helmet before he collapsed.

Raig let out a loud roar and took the other soldier's head off. Rue stopped for a brief moment to draw in a breath. Raig stumbled, then hit his knees.

Rue caught him.

Around them, the battle seemed to be waning, but all Rue saw was the blood filling Raig's mouth and spilling from the corners of his lips.

"No… Don't you dare leave me!"

Raig smiled, and more blood pooled in Rue's palm where he cradled his lover's head. "I will always love you."

Rue bent to kiss him. "Please…"

When he looked at his beloved knight's face, the light that had always been in those beautiful eyes faded. Teardrops wet Raig's beard, and Rue held him tight.

"Until we meet again, my love," he whispered.

* * *

Elijah missed his shot, hitting the tree beside Mirov's horse. He spun around, only to see Rue clutching Raig as blood poured out of the man's neck. Rue rocked and shook his head, whispering.

Another arrow whizzed by Elijah's head, and he grabbed Sarin to tug the man down. "We have to take out the last of those archers!"

Sarin nodded. He and Elijah returned to their positions and rejoined the fight, making quick work of the few remaining enemy archers.

By the time the last arrow found its target and the last fireball hit the ground, Mirov stood in a sea of bloodied bodies, with only a few men remaining.

"Mirov!" Aven bellowed from where he stood on the wall. Hair disheveled, scratches on his face, he looked like every warrior Elijah had ever read about. "Lay down your weapon!"

Mirov smirked. "And watch you put my bitch of a sister on the throne?" He drew a knife. Elijah readied his bow, should Mirov do something stupid. "I will die first!"

Elijah gasped as Mirov slit his own throat. Blood gushed out and onto the man's horse. The horse panicked and threw Mirov's body off before bolting into the woods. Mirov's last men tossed their weapons to the ground. Aven left the wall with several men, Elsbeth behind them. Soldiers gathered Mirov's men and bound their arms before leading them away. Elsbeth stood at her brother's body.

"It's over," she said, loud enough for others to hear. She smiled up at the wall. "It's over!"

Cheers erupted, but Elijah didn't care. He and Sarin rushed back into the keep where Rue had taken Raig. On one of the tables in the great hall, Raig lay motionless. Rue sat beside him, Raig's hand gripped tightly in his own. Tears flowed down Rue's cheeks. When Sarin held his father, Rue cried.

Elijah swallowed, unable to stop his own tears from escaping. Raig had been Rue's lover for ages. He'd been a brave, wonderful man. Elijah walked up and bent to kiss Raig's forehead. Then he sat on the other side of Sarin, listening to his lover and Rue cry softly.

* * *

Numb, Sarin watched his father light Raig's pyre. Rue hadn't spoken since the small memorial service Elsbeth had conducted. They lost many people, but none of those felt like this. Raig had been a second father, a beloved friend. And Sarin worried for Rue's wellbeing.

Arms slipped around Sarin's waist, and he rested one hand on Elijah's. They'd both been wounded, but only minor injuries. Others had fared worse.

"Has he said anything?"

Sarin shook his head. "Nothing."

Elijah sighed. "I wish... God, Sarin, I'd give anything to bring Raig back."

"So would I."

The fire quickly engulfed Raig's body and the red rose clutched in his lifeless hands. Rue stared at it long after others paid their respects and left. Sarin and Elijah remained as well. When Rue finally turned to them, Sarin saw no hint of the happiness he'd known in his father's eyes. It was as if Rue died alongside his lover.

Sarin wanted to speak, but he couldn't make the words come out. When Rue did, what he said didn't really surprise Sarin.

"I am leaving."

"Where will you go?" Elijah asked.

"I don't know," Rue answered, his tone flat, lifeless. "I'm an old man. Should Laenasse decide it's my time, then so be it. She will claim me when she is ready to do so." He gave them both a shaky smile. "Care for one another. Never let anything tear you apart."

Sarin stepped out of Elijah's arms and into his father's. Eyes closing, he fought back more tears. "I love you," he whispered.

"You..." Rue swallowed, and his voice broke for a moment. "You would make any man proud to be a father. I love you so much, Sarin."

When Rue stepped back, he drew Elijah into a tight embrace. "Take care of him," he whispered.

"Always."

After a few moments, they followed Rue to the stables. Elijah stood nearby while Sarin helped Rue secure the two packs to the horse's saddle. A part of him hadn't been too surprised when Rue announced he was leaving, but it didn't make things feel better. Rue had become the father Elijah wished he'd had all his life. Watching Rue leave -- watching Sarin fight the heartache -- made Elijah hate Mirov more than he ever thought possible.

Rue swung up into the saddle and gathered the reins. "You will be fine," he said. "Both of you."

"Will we ever see you again?" Elijah asked.

"I don't know," Rue said. "But know that I love you both very much. Elijah, you have become a son to me. I trust you to protect Sarin, and he you, until the ends of your days."

"Love you, too," Elijah said. He took Sarin's hand as the mage stepped back to him.

"May Laenasse guide you," Sarin said.

Rue nodded. "And you." With that, he headed out of the front gate, out of their lives.

* * *

Elijah gave Sarin's hand a gentle squeeze.

"I'm all right. He will be, too. I'd do anything to take the pain from him, but he will handle it how he feels he needs to."

"Do you think we'll ever see him again?"

Sarin shrugged. "I have no idea. I hope so. He's my father, and, despite being old, he still has a long time before I think Laenasse will call him to her side."

Elijah let go of Sarin's hand and put his arm around the mage's shoulders. "Come on, love. I'm sure everyone's wondering where we are. Did Rue tell anyone else he's leaving?"

"Aven and Elsbeth know," Sarin said as they walked toward the keep. "Our order is known for such things, so Rue's leaving won't be a shock to anyone."

"He was the historian -- the seer. Who will do that now?"

Sarin gave him a small smile. "You're looking at him."

"I had the feeling you'd say that."

They entered the keep. Despite the victory and Nathan's pending coronation, the mood remained somber. Most of the order had left already, back to wherever they came from. The wounded had been moved to another section of the keep where healers could tend to them without distractions. Several long tables filled the great hall, and servants were setting out what promised to be an amazing feast.

"He is gone then?" Aven asked when he met Sarin and Elijah halfway.

"He is." Sarin smiled as Aven gave his shoulder a squeeze.

"Rue is a dear friend and a strong mage," Elsbeth said, joining them. "I do not think this is the last we will see of him."

"Do you wish to retire for a while before the banquet and coronation?" Aven asked.

"Honestly..." Sarin sighed. "I need the distraction. I need laughter and happiness."

Aven grinned. "Then join us." He clapped his hands, and a servant rang a loud bell. All those still in the great hall gathered. "My friends! We have experienced heartbreak and the horrors of war, but we have also experienced victory over an evil that has imprisoned this land."

Everyone cheered, and the sound was more welcome than Elijah could ever begin to explain.

"We also have a king to crown!" Elsbeth announced.

Looking far more confident than he had before,

Nathan approached his mother where she stood on the dais in front of a single throne. He knelt on one knee, head bowed. Elsbeth took a golden crown from the purple pillow Aven held out to her. She placed the crown on Nathan's head.

"People of Timiria, I, Elsbeth Aevail, daughter of kings, hereby abdicate my throne to Nathan Aevail, son of Aven Daesya and myself. May he rule with kindness and prosperity."

Nathan stood and turned slowly.

The applause thundered in the great hall. Elijah clapped alongside Sarin and Braden, who beamed with so much pride, he looked like he would burst. Nathan held up a hand, and the room soon fell silent.

"Thank you. I do not know what sort of king I will be, but I swear to you -- people of Timiria -- that I will do my best. My first decree as king is one that is close to my heart for many reasons. From this day forward, magic is no longer outlawed. Mages will have the same freedom, the same protections, that others enjoy. No one will be imprisoned or executed for their magic unless they use it to harm another."

More people than Elijah expected let out shouts of joy. He smiled at Sarin.

"Furthermore," Nathan said when the din died down. "Given the memories and nightmares of Mirov's rule from Cosei, I am moving the royal residence to Pelarum. We will rebuild, and everyone will prosper."

* * *

"That was more of a speech than I expected," Elijah said with a grin.

Nathan laughed and leaned back against Braden. Around them, the tables were filled with people celebrating, chatting, eating, drinking. The mood, once somber, now seemed brighter, hopeful.

"I wrote it all down," Nathan said. He dug in his pocket and handed Elijah a folded bit of paper.

Elijah chuckled as he read it. Everything, word for word, had been written. "How are you feeling?"

"Honestly?" Nathan glanced around, then leaned forward, voice lowering to a whisper. "Terrified."

Braden smiled. "You aren't alone, though."

"Nope." Nathan relaxed once more. "How about you two?"

Elijah let Sarin answer.

"Better," Sarin said. "I miss him, but I know he'll be fine."

"So..." Elijah said. "Do we call you 'Your Highness' now?"

Nathan shuddered. "Please, gods, not in private. I guess, in public, it's kind of necessary, but in private, I'm just Nathan."

A fork clinked against a metal cup, and Aven stood. "My friends, my king," he said with a bow toward Nathan, "in front of you all, I would like to ask Elsbeth Aevail for her hand in marriage."

Elsbeth's eyes widen, and she gasped. "Really?" she whispered in the almost-deafening silence.

Aven smiled and went down on one knee. He held out a glimmering ring of gold. "Will you marry me?"

"Yes!"

Cheers erupted as she jumped up and into his arms.

"Don't know about you," Sarin whispered in Elijah's ear, "but I need a break."

They said their goodbyes and left the revelers to celebrate the impending wedding.

Once in the bedroom, door shut on the noise, Elijah sighed. The silence felt peaceful and calming. Until lips touched his own.

Elijah opened to the kiss, arms going around Sarin's neck. They'd been through hell and back, and all he wanted now was to remind himself why returning to his version of Earth would never, ever happen.

"Make love to me?" Sarin murmured.

"You never need to ask."

Elijah walked them to the bed, tugging Sarin's tunic off on the way. His own joined it on the floor, followed by boots and pants. Sarin stretched out on the bed, cock hard, furred thighs open. Elijah crawled between them and bent to lick Sarin from base to tip. Sarin moaned softly, arching.

Elijah would have happily remained where he was, but Sarin's moans and writhing went straight to his cock. Elijah scooted up and found the oil they used as lube. He coated two fingers and reached down to ease them into Sarin's body.

"Yes…" Sarin hissed softly. "Need you."

"You have me." Elijah withdrew his fingers and pushed his cock in until his body rested against Sarin's. "Always."

Nodding, Sarin speared his fingers through Elijah's hair and tugged Elijah down for a kiss. Elijah swallowed the mage's gasps and moans as he began stroking in and out, slow and easy. Every breath Sarin exhaled made Elijah want the man even more, especially after all they'd been through. Elijah caught Sarin's hands and laced their fingers together. Pressing Sarin's hands up onto the bed, Elijah sped up.

"Gods," Sarin panted. "Yes. Love…"

Sarin's orgasm hit with little warning. He cried

out, warmth spreading between them. Elijah groaned and buried his face in the mage's long hair as his own washed through him.

They stayed like that for a moment, just breathing.

"I don't know what magic brought me here," Elijah murmured. "But I'm glad it did."

Sarin hugged him tight. "As am I, love. As am I."

Vocabulary of the Timiria

Laenasse priesthood:
I ruqa aeui. -- I love you.
Eorsr omd ksuma, raad kae corr. -- Earth and stone, heed my call.
Ikvada uir amakeak. -- Impede our enemies.

Orc:
Karr han! -- Kill him!
Shave availkord, davulk! -- Show yourself, coward!
Tholo avai ulo, vhork! -- There you are, whelp!
Ukorokk daark. I varr karr avai navkord! -- Useless fools. I will kill you myself!

Mychael Black

Myc has been writing professionally since 2005, solo and with Shayne Carmichael. Genres include pretty much anything (no steampunk yet), though Myc is well known for paranormal stories. When not writing, Myc is usually playing PC games, reading, watching Netflix, and spending way too much time on Facebook. Since the question has come up in the past, pronouns are not an issue. Myc is bio-female, mentally male, and 100% genderfluid, so any pronoun works!

"Black's work is poetic and haunting. Nobody can pull off smoldering sex alongside holler-deep, soulful characters like Mychael Black." --Sara Jay

Mychael at Changeling: changelingpress.com/mychael-black-a-128

Changeling Press E-Books

More Sci-Fi, Fantasy, Paranormal, and BDSM adventures available in e-book format for immediate download at ChangelingPress.com -- Werewolves, Vampires, Dragons, Shapeshifters and more -- Erotic Tales from the edge of your imagination.

What are E-Books?

E-books, or electronic books, are books designed to be read in digital format -- on your desktop or laptop computer, notebook, tablet, Smart Phone, or any electronic e-book reader.

Where can I get Changeling Press E-Books?

Changeling Press e-books are available at ChangelingPress.com, Amazon, Apple Books, Barnes & Noble, and Kobo/Walmart.

ChangelingPress.com